FLIGHT
OF THE
SPARROW

JULIA CUNNINGHAM was born in Spokane, Washington. She attended a variety of schools, but considers herself self-educated. Although there was a time when she hoped to be a painter or a musician, she has found that words suit her best. Miss Cunningham lived in seven states and France before settling in Santa Barbara, California where she now lives and writes.

FLIGHT OF THE SPARROW

BY JULIA
CUNNINGHAM

AN AVON  CAMELOT BOOK

AVON BOOKS
A division of
The Hearst Corporation
959 Eighth Avenue
New York, New York 10019

First Camelot Printing, April, 1982

The Pantheon Books edition contains the following Library of
Congress Cataloging in Publication Data:

Cunningham, Julia. Flight of the sparrow.
Summary: After stealing a valuable painting for the
band of street urchins who have adopted her, a ten-
year-old orphan must flee Paris. [1. Orphans—Fiction.
2. Gangs—Fiction. 3. Poverty—Fiction. 4. France—
Fiction] I. Title.
PZ7.C9167F1 [Fic] 80-12788

6th grade reading level has been determined by using the Fry
Readability Scale.

Cover illustration by Norman Walker

For Katy Peake

FOR HER CREATIVE GENEROSITY,
A GIVING BEYOND THE GIFT,
AND FOR HERSELF
WITH UNWORDED LOVE

FLIGHT
OF THE
SPARROW

One

I AM TELLING MY STORY not for myself but for Mago. There is space between what I was and what I am and all because of him. It started like this.

My first remembering is murky, but it smelled very sweet. Too sweet maybe, like an overdose of cheap perfume, the kind you get in slot machines. But a person of three years can not tell what is too much or too little. She just enjoys or doesn't. I did. I think the sweetness was a woman. Maybe my mother, though I never met anyone to call that, then or later.

But sometimes when the early morning frost got to me from the toes up, I sniffed the memory. It canceled out the dank stones under the bridge where I slept when I couldn't find a better surface. It even muffled the more pungent sweats and sournesses of my comrades—from Mago, who shared his bread with me when he had any, to Eel, who was tolerated only because he could slip through grilled gates and slightly raised windows too narrow for the rest of us to pass.

Maybe, instead of beginning with myself, I'll start with how I met Mago.

I was nine then, one year before now where I am ten.

I'd just been imprisoned in my second orphanage. The first I don't remember because I'd been adopted out of it right away, only that didn't work because I became sick and they got rid of me by leaving me in a hospital corridor. But all that has no colors. That house was gray with dirt and gloom, and the hospital was white, so that's all anyone has to know about them. The second orphanage was as though the bricks had been dipped in old blood, if one can count that a color, and the inside was a green so dark it could be called black. But one thing was all rainbow. One person. The boy who delivered the laundry caught me crying in the furnace room and hauled me up by my armpits and propped me against the cement wall and then let me have it. With words.

The words came out right, the way a good song does that can be whispered or shouted in time to the tap of a foot or the blow of the wind.

"Listen, little street sparrow, don't ever cry again," he said, his green eyes so close I could have counted the lashes around them. "The land of tears is not for you and me. It's a soft place where you sit on cushions and get fed every day. It's a house that's clean. It's good clothes on Sunday and shoes all year round. We're strangers there, and no use to knock on that door. The street's our home, where our garden's an alley and the fireplace a garbage can. Our bed is where we find it, and we collect old sacks to cover us. I want you to hear me, and what you don't know I'll teach you."

"Why me?" I asked, astounded that this tall, flickering candle of a boy was bothering with the sodden weed I was.

"Because I like you and you need somebody," he said

4

flatly without any weakness. "I'll be your brother—if the idea comes easy to you. I'm Mago. What do you call yourself?"

I knew that he was going to let me join him, that he would take me away from the orphanage. And his colors were so bright that I wanted to start new and maybe someday mine would be too.

"I just threw it away," I said. Already I didn't have to explain.

He laughed, and the way his eyes lighted his face brought the rainbow right around me. "You're not very tough yet," he said, inspecting how I looked. "Try this." He drew the stub of a cigarette from behind his ear and put it gently behind mine. He laughed again. "That's good. You're more like me now. I'll call you Little Cigarette, and when you're taller I'll drop the 'Little,' but that's a long day from here."

We crept out of the cellar window, Mago and me together.

In those days Mago shared a rickety garden shed back of a twenty-story apartment house on the outskirts of Paris. He shared the tiny space with a pale, sickly girl named Friquette—who resented my coming and later drowned herself in the Seine because she knew she was dying—and a strange boy shaped like a stump, who was retarded. His name was Drollant, and sometimes he really was droll. He loved best to go to the zoo, and that very day, my first, we took him there.

I'd never been, and I stared at the elephants so long Mago said I'd turn into one. That's when I began to learn to laugh. I mean, how would I have looked with a trunk instead of a nose? Mago said I was being childish. But then he laughed too, and we didn't stop until we were in front of the tigers' cage.

Then I saw another Mago. He went right up to them, eye to eye, and talked—but in a kind of humming with no words. And those tigers must have understood. They both sat down and purred at him.

Drollant poked his hands between the bars, and that stopped what was going on.

Mago was angry. "You know better than that!" he scolded his friend and slapped Drollant's wrists hard.

Drollant looked very ashamed and raced off to where some seals were rolling around in a pond.

I should have kept what I was feeling silent, but I said, "You hurt him."

Mago looked suddenly very old, though he was only about thirteen. "One day I won't be with him." And that was all he said.

I figured out what he meant. That the world is full of tigers, all kinds, and Drollant might someday end up skinned like a rabbit in the butcher shop, not knowing why or even how. It came to me then that Mago was very wise. I've never changed my mind.

On the way back Friquette, who hadn't said a word the whole afternoon, just watching Mago and me, lagged behind. Mago motioned me ahead with Drollant so I couldn't see how they looked as the two of them talked, but I could hear plenty. Friquette's voice, pitched purposely high, made it easy.

"Why'd you take in that little mouse? She's no good to anybody."

"Because she needs us."

"Give her another two years and you'll see. She'll need nobody, not even you. Wish I could count on being here to see the proof of it."

Her words broke off into coughing, hard, dry heaves that must have bruised her ribs. I wanted to turn and ask her what she had against me, but the answer came a minute after I'd wished for it.

Mago did the asking. "Why don't you try to like Cigarette?"

The coughing stopped abruptly. Friquette's tones became as bitter as winter. "You know I was getting better until that little leech fastened on to you. It's making me sick just to look at her."

"Oh, Friquette!" Mago's words were said on a sigh, and when I did glance behind I saw that he had encircled her with his left arm as they walked and that she had rested her head on his shoulder.

All that was the beginning of my new life.

Two

THOSE FIRST DAYS AND NIGHTS were like living in the middle of an amusement park. Very early each morning, even before the sky lighted up, the colors were there. We'd sit around in that little shed that smelled of fertilizer and eat what we had, Mago, Drollant, Friquette, and me, and then mostly Mago and I would set out into the city. As we became enclosed in the buildings, the trees, and the people Mago would often say, "It's like a theater, something dramatic happening every minute."

On quiet mornings I'd ask him what was "dramatic"— and of course I'd never been inside a theater—about the old woman selling papers or the boy sweeping the gutters with a twig broom.

"If you were inside their heads, you'd know what I mean," he would answer.

"Are *you*?" I asked him, just once and never again. He turned a look on me that almost cut me off from the living. That look was a fence higher than the bridges that crossed the Seine. For that instant I wasn't anybody, wasn't even there.

Mago was just different, and I had to learn that the

8

same way you learn that you're never going to get to see a circus or live in a château.

Anyway, as I said so many words ago, those first times were good times. But in my happiness I had forgotten one thing—winter.

It was a bad one that year, and it began just before the frost came, with Friquette killing herself. Drollant saw her do it.

Mago and I were sitting around a little fire we'd lit behind the toolshed. It was after midnight and safe enough from anyone in the apartment house seeing us.

Suddenly Drollant stumbled into the circle of firelight and fell against me, nearly knocking me over.

I wasn't too patient. "What's the matter with you now?" I snapped at him.

He stared at me a moment as if he didn't recognize me and then began his blubbering kind of crying.

It took Mago to calm him down. He did it by rubbing his back in long, light strokes, and at last Drollant could talk.

"I saw the splash, Mago, I saw the splash," he began.

"In the river?" said Mago very quietly.

Drollant nodded.

"Who fell in?"

"Friquette."

"Did she swim to the bank?"

"No. She didn't want to."

"How do you know that?"

"Because she jumped in all by herself."

"Did you get anybody to help?"

"I didn't have to. Really, I didn't, Mago!"

Mago was holding the boy in his arms now.

"Who came?" was all he asked.

"First two women who saw too, and then three police-men."

"Did you see Friquette again?" His voice was so gentle I had to strain to hear him.

"Yes. I waited."

"Did she speak to you?"

"No. She couldn't. She was dead. Her eyes were stones. Then I ran to find you."

Mago got up and carried Drollant into the shed and put him down on his own bed and covered him with sacking, mine and his, to warm the trembling out of him. Then he drew me outside and whispered, "She was too sick to get well. We'll say prayers for her tomorrow. Go to sleep now and don't dream."

But it was a long time before I closed my eyes. I kept thinking about Friquette and forgave her for hating me. But she wasn't there to forgive, so I had to forgive myself for hating her back.

That next morning there was darkness where there should have been dawn, and the one grimy window was all frosted over. I got up first and opened the door. Like a thin, white, covering sheet, it was spread over all the gardens and the little plots of grass. The chill pinched my face and hands.

I hoped Friquette was warm where she was, though dead has always meant dead to me ever since a cat I knew in the orphanage got hit by a car and left in an alley. He was stiff, like he'd never been limp. His catness had completely disappeared.

Mago was getting Drollant up now. "We're moving into the city today," he said to both of us, "before all the good places are gone."

10

"Good places" meant nothing to me until we started to look for one. Three hours later we'd found it, or rather Mago·had, a kind of cave of a room a floor above the street in a neighborhood of rotted houses that had been abandoned by everybody but roamers like us. The two windows were without any panes, but Mago said sacks would take care of that. And rats had chewed some holes through the walls and floor, but Mago said we'd stuff the holes with stones wrapped in newspaper to keep them out.

What made it real was the fireplace. The mantel had lost its marble top except for one triangle still cemented onto a corner, and the little rim of plaster grapes was chipped so that only one bunch was whole—but what was left was pretty. I ran my fingers over the tiny rounds and the cracked stems, and soon Drollant started doing it too.

"Drollant," Mago said, "you're to stay here until we get back."

The boy's mouth drooped, and he began to whimper.

"No, you don't understand," continued Mago. "You are in charge. If anyone comes, tell them your gang is due any minute and they're to go away. Get that?"

Drollant's face was now almost normal with delight. He puffed out his chest like a pigeon and nodded.

I didn't know where we were going, but Mago did. He walked so fast I had to trot to keep up. We wound in and out of streets I wished I could stroll through, but I soon caught on. We were heading for a very tall building that had two towers just across the river. But before we got there, Mago stopped at the edge of a block that was filled with flower stalls.

"Now listen carefully," he said. "I want you to go over to

that fat woman in the green sweater. See? The one in front of all those potted plants. You're to ask her how much that little one is with the pink flowers growing in it. When she gives you a price, you will argue with her, keep her talking. Agreed?"

"But why?"

"I'm teaching you something, Little Cigarette." He was very patient with me, the way he was with Drollant. "Just do as I tell you."

I obeyed him. I always did.

I stammered a little but managed to ask the price of the plant.

The woman looked down at me as though I were crazy. "What's that to you?" she said, turning to arrange a row of pots.

I asked her again.

This time she was cross. "If you have the money to buy a stringbean I'd be surprised enough to believe in miracles. Off with you!"

I could see I was failing Mago. I had to do something, so I kicked her leg.

She bent down to rub the hurting with one hand and grabbed for me with the other. "You little devil!" she shrieked. "I'll have you arrested!"

But I was too quick for her, and as I darted backward I gave two pots a shove with my arm. They crashed onto the pavement.

Her curses brought her company, and she was immediately surrounded by a crowd. That was my chance to escape, and I did, looking hurriedly around for Mago. I saw him where we had first paused. He signaled for me to follow him. We both raced like hounds out of the market and over the bridge to the other side.

It wasn't until we stood, panting, under the shadow of that stone building with the towers that I noticed his arms were filled with flowers.

"Where did you get them?" I gasped.

He just grinned, and I realized my question had been foolish. While I was distracting the pot woman, he had snatched the flowers from another stall.

He patted my shoulder. "You did well," he said.

I was very proud.

Then Mago got so solemn he was almost a stranger. He seemed to forget me as he walked slowly into the building that had a door as wide as an oak tree.

The darkness of the inside struck me blind for a moment. Then out of the dimness appeared hundreds of lighted candles on both sides under high arches. I looked upward as Mago was doing, and a deeper shock hit me. Windows! Colors! Blazing colors!

"Oh, Mago!"

He looked at me and quickly supported my right arm as if he were afraid I was going to faint. "It's all right, Little Cigarette. Blink hard. They're glass of long ago." He pointed to the round one far away in front of us. "See? It's a rose."

I saw and drew in some deep breaths so that I could see some more. I think I must have toured that weird place fifteen times, always staring up, sometimes stumbling against the benches that filled the center part before I could make myself come back down from them.

Mago had waited, and now he took my elbow and led

me to one of the candled places that was like an open room, missing one wall. He sat me on a bench and then took his flowers up to a statue and laid them at its plaster feet. He stood there a few minutes as though he were talking to the tall lady before him, painted blue and white. She couldn't answer back, but I watched Mago's head nodding as though she were.

When he came back, his eyes held something I had never noticed there before—sadness, sadness like the end of the world.

He slid onto the seat beside me and for a long time was so alone I didn't dare talk to him.

At last he turned to me and smiled, and the sadness was gone. "The flowers were for Friquette," he said.

"But you gave them to the lady," I couldn't help saying.

"She'll tell Friquette I left them for her."

I couldn't understand how this would be possible since the lady was not real and Friquette was a cold body in the morgue, but if Mago believed this I would try to believe it too. After all, he was wise and I wasn't.

With one final bow to his statue, he started out. I followed, after filling myself once more with those upper windows so bright I knew I would be able to see them in my head over and over whenever I wanted to.

When we were on the street again, the smell of bread layered the air. "I'm hungry," I said, keeping my voice small so that he could pretend not to hear it if he wished. I knew he had no money.

"Me too," he replied cheerfully. "Want a stuffed chicken with mushrooms, or maybe ham and bacon on cooked cabbage with beer to wash it down?"

He sort of challenged me to laugh, and I did. Just being

with him, with someone to care whether I ate or not, made laughing easy.

"We must take something back to Drollant too," he murmured very thoughtfully. "Tell you what, Little Cigarette. Your training starts right now. Do you know what 'doleful' means?"

I shook my head.

He pulled the corners of his mouth downward and lifted his eyebrows as he sucked in his cheeks. "That's doleful," he said. "You try it."

I imitated him, and he clapped me on the back. "First rate! You're a very quick learner. Now limp a bit, not too much, just so it looks like it hurts."

I added a limp.

"Now hold out your hands and make them shake a little. You're sick of a fever and too soon out of bed. Understood?"

I understood so well that a woman passing by muttered "Poor little soul" and then dug out a few coins from her handbag and put them into my palm. I almost dropped them in my excitement but managed a hurried "Thank you" before she left.

I could tell Mago was very pleased with me, but just then he began to sing. The song was as sad as his face had been when he was discussing Friquette with the lady, and very soon people began to stop and listen.

When he finished, there was a clinking of more coins on the cobblestones. He bowed all around and signaled to me to pick them up. I forgot my limp and scurried like a rat after cheese until I had them safe in my one pocket. I held on to the pocket very tightly, afraid our riches might vanish.

15

Mago beckoned me into the bakery where the good smells came from and bought a long loaf, which he tucked under one arm. Next we went to another shop and came out with a large hunk of yellow cheese. The last stop was for three red apples. I carried the cheese, and Mago stuffed the apples into his pockets.

What a feast we had, Mago and me and Drollant, in our little room, with singing afterward. Drollant couldn't carry a tune, but the sound he made wasn't unpleasant, like a big bee. And this was when I started to learn Mago's songs.

"When you're good enough," he said, "we'll take different corners. That way we'll earn double."

How happy I was that night as I crawled in under my sacks! And my dreams were windows, red and yellow, blue and scarlet, purple and green, all shining down on me.

Three

AT THE BEGINNING I mentioned a person called Eel, so narrow that he could squeeze through a sewer grid. His name fitted him, which I guess is why he had it. He was also very slippery—his nature, I mean—and I was sorry one evening to find him in our room. He'd been gone for some weeks.

"Wondered where you were off to," Mago greeted him. "Thought of leaving you a note in the shed but then I remembered you couldn't read."

Eel hiked up his shoulders arrogantly. "No profit in reading where I've been."

When he failed to add where that was, Mago said nothing. I had discovered that questions weren't welcome in this class of society, but I figured Eel's former shelter might have been a prison because even for Eel his skin was too pale.

Mago offered his guest the last of the cheese and half a glass of wine, and Eel practically swallowed it all whole. He wiped his mouth on his sleeve and then hunkered down before the fireplace. He didn't add to its elegance, and if I'd been Mago I would have told him to go. God knows I wish now he had. Eel was about to cast the first shadow on my new life.

I knew this even before he spoke, but his words made it clear.

"There's a golden apple waiting to be plucked," he said, very pleased with his own language.

Mago chuckled. "Can't eat gold," he said, showing no curiosity.

Drollant giggled just because Mago was amused.

Eel swiveled to face Drollant. "Still got the idiot with you? I'd tie him to a cart and use him like a horse if he were mine."

Drollant, not really understanding but aware that something had been spoken against him, started his sniveling.

Mago got up and stood over Eel. "Drollant is my friend," was all he said.

Eel backed down quickly. "Well, he's no concern of mine."

"That's correct," said Mago, stern as a stone lion. "Keep it that way."

Eel now tried to retrieve Mago's favor. "Don't you want to hear what I have in mind?"

"Maybe."

I wished right then that I could just erase Eel from the room. He carried trouble on his back as surely as if a hump grew there. But Mago was his own master, and I was just someone who walked in his footsteps.

Eel glanced at me. "Can she be trusted?" he asked. I might have been a cockroach only there was a peculiar shrewdness behind his question.

"She belongs here," was Mago's answer.

18

"Then I'll get to it." He lowered his voice, though there was no one to listen except us and the rise of wind outside our cloth-covered windows.

"I've been spying on somebody. He lives in a loft on the Rue Cigale and he paints." Eel paused as though he had said something of importance.

"Paints what?" said Mago, yawning. "Walls? Houses? Pictures?"

"Himself, mostly," answered Eel, still choosing to be mysterious even if none of us was interested in looking for clues. We three just waited somewhat sleepily. "I mean," he continued, "he shows up at the café splotched with daubs of color all over his clothes. Sometimes they even reach to his beard."

Eel scrubbed at his ears with the flat of his hands as though they itched, and then, as if this motion had sharpened his already sharp-edged brain, he arrived at the point.

"In this man's studio is a painting by a famous artist. Forget his name, something like Manfred. Seen his things in museums. How my little pigeon got hold of it, who knows? Maybe he was left it by a rich uncle. But however, it's worth a château in Normandy."

"You ever see it?" Mago was getting drowsy.

"Once. He lent it for a week to the man up the street who runs that little gallery where the limousines stop. Can't myself see what all the fuss is about. Just a picture of a woman in a green dress. But here's how we come in. Monsieur Flan, the gallery owner, wants that painting so fierce—he could retire on the profit he'd make selling it—he'd trade his right leg for it."

"How do you know all this?"

"Heard him make an offer to Monsieur Michel." Eel glimpsed my bewilderment. "The artist," he added, not too kindly. "Was turned down—flat."

"This painter rich?" asked Mago.

Eel snorted. "Not likely. He's poor as we are."

"So?"

"So what Flan wants he pays for, and no outside questions. With a minimum of intelligent planning we can get it for him and be paid. Clear?"

"As clay," said Mago. "Why don't you just go ahead and do it? Why try for partners?"

"Because," said Eel, his face forward, quivering like a rat who has smelled good garbage, "I'm marked. Flan knows the police sort of keep a watch on me. I've been in the lockup more than once, and he wouldn't take a chance being seen buying a painting off me if I walked in with one."

"And you figure he'll buy it from me all dressed up in my pin-stripe pants and tail coat?"

"You go in his back door with that wrapped in newspaper, and he'll grab it. He'll sell it the same way, through somebody else's back door."

Mago sat back, his whole attitude skeptical. "So then?" he muttered, and this is where the bad part began.

"So you've got an innocent living here we can use."

"Drollant?" said Mago, surprised out of his tiredness.

"Hah! Better a day-old sparrow! No—the girl."

I might have been a life-sized cardboard cutout for all he really cared who or what I was. People like Eel only see other people as targets for taking, and if they give, it's more apt to be a knife in the gut than a handful of roses.

Mago was really awake now. He was gazing at me as if

he were trying to see my thoughts printed on my forehead. When he finally spoke, his voice was gentle and just for me. "Do you want to?" he said, and I knew that if I answered no he wouldn't hold it against me, not for one second.

"I don't know," was what came out of my insides. I couldn't help it. I really didn't know.

"Then that's all for now," said Mago, and he got up.

"Okay," said Eel, taking the hint and starting to leave. "We'll wait till she does." He sort of slithered through the partly open door like a snake in the zoo.

Mago and I talked together until late that night while Drollant snored in his corner, and Mago never once threw his opinions into the conversation; he just drew out mine.

I told him I'd never stolen anything before, anything that was of much more value than twenty or thirty francs, about enough to buy food for a few days or a pair of rope shoes in the market. I told him I was afraid to risk my freedom, that the woman who'd owned me when I was small used to shut me up in a chest and then bang on the lid until I screamed.

I got sort of shivery telling him this, and he came and sat very close beside me, like he was protecting me from what I was remembering. In that moment I loved him forever.

And when I came to the end of my telling—the night just beginning to move off and be day—I turned to him and said, "No."

He smiled, and we both got under our sacks and slept.

Four

THE TERRIBLE THING that happened the next day was my fault. When we woke up that morning, Drollant had one of his fits. They didn't come often, but when they did, he had to be taken out and walked fast. Mago explained that Drollant sometimes went into a panic when he was inside a walled place. He was going sort of wild, swinging his arms like windmills as if he were trying to clear a space around him. A stream of blubbery noises was pouring from his slack mouth. But his eyes were the worst. They were blank, blank with terror.

"Get on his other side!" Mago ordered, taking hold of Drollant by his right arm.

Together we propelled him out into the street, sort of lifting him along, his feet sometimes touching the cobblestones, sometimes kicking the air as though there were a barricade in front of him.

But when he began to grunt, Mago gestured to me to let him down onto a park bench that was near us. Drollant sat pretty straight with only frequent and senseless nods of his head.

"He's coming out of it," said Mago, "but he needs to be watched for a while yet. You sit here with him, and I'll go get him one of those sugar sticks he likes. Be back soon."

I wish now I had stopped Mago from going—the whole miserable mess that came later would never have happened—but who knows about tomorrow today?

Anyway, we sat there, and Drollant was still nodding as though he had a broken spring in his neck. And as people passing by us began to pause and make comments—"He should be in some place where he's taken care of" and "It's a disgrace what's on the street these days"—I wasn't too happy to be seen with him. Truthfully, I was ashamed, and at the same time sorry I was.

So when a very stout woman loomed up over me and shook her fat finger in my face and said, "Take that idiot home or I'll call someone who will," I lost whatever good self should have punched her in the belly, telling her to mind her own business.

Instead, God help me, I looked up at her with a smile so false my cheeks hurt and said, "He's nothing to me. He's just sitting here."

"Not any longer he isn't," she boomed back and grabbed poor Drollant by the elbow and heaved him upright. "I'll take you where you belong, to an asylum!" she shouted at Drollant.

He must have understood. He flung himself free of her and darted wildly up the walk and into the traffic that circled the park. There was a shriek of brakes, a thud, and Drollant went down.

When the ambulance came and took him away, I did nothing. Who would have listened to me, a dirty little nobody? I stayed frozen to that bench until Mago showed up and then he had to shake me hard to start me talking. Somehow I got out the truth, all of it.

23

Mago seemed to ignore everything except his repeated question, "Where did they take him?"

I was crying by now and could only shake my head.

"What was written on the ambulance?" he insisted.

I wiped my eyes on my sleeve and tried to see again the high, black letters that had been on the van.

"You've got to remember!"

"I can't!"

"You can!"

And I could. I spelled them out, and Mago put them together.

Mago let out his breath through his front teeth. "That's the city hospital! It's where you go to die. We street people all end up there."

His strength seemed to drain from him, and now it was my turn to take charge. I forgot my tears and led him back to our room like a bewildered dog on a rope.

I knew I had to pull Mago from the pit he was in. Without him I was nothing and might as well be lying beside Drollant, my last breaths rattling from my chest.

My beginning was feeble. "Maybe he isn't dying. Maybe he just broke his leg or bruised his back."

Mago let his head droop so low I couldn't see his face. He was muttering phrases that were so muffled I caught only broken pieces of them: "—seen them, seen them— no hope—scared to go."

"I'll go with you," I said, trying to make sense from his words.

His head came up, and he stared at me as though it were the first time he had ever seen me. I shook him by the shoulders to erase the strangeness from his eyes, and suddenly they clicked back to seeing right.

He spoke. "He has to die sometime, maybe sooner than you or me, but not there. Not in that hell where what's in the bed is a body. Alive or dead, not someone but a body. I know. I've been there." He shuddered.

"Was something wrong with you?" Anything to keep him with me, not adrift in that kind of shock he was emerging from.

"Not me. The man who used to call me his son. And I called him father. I wasn't. He wasn't. But the pretending was real. He died in that place."

I could see that Mago was so stamped with despair, that I'd have to be the strong one, if only this once. I pulled at his arms until I got him standing, and he looked down at me with a half-question that didn't much care about hearing the answer.

When we were on the street and walking, I told him, "We're going to visit Drollant."

He didn't pull back but shortened his steps to match mine exactly, as if he were tied to my legs and had to be attached so he could move.

In some ways I was grateful that Mago was only half himself because that hospital wasn't a picnic in a park. From the first twenty minutes of waiting at the reception desk to find out where they had put Drollant, the smells and the misery of the people crowding the benches, some with grimy bandages on them, others so pinched and pale they could have been dead already, clamped down on me like being dipped in pig wallow.

Going upstairs—someone whose face was swollen up with sourness gave us the number of the ward—was a relief, and the ward itself with its long lines of beds on each side of the room offered more breathing space.

We found Drollant at the far end, in one corner. He had pulled the sheet up over his head, but we recognized his stubby shape under the covers. Mago's smile at the sight of Drollant's surprise as he peered from the rumple of whiteness was himself come back.

"Ho, there!" he said to the invalid. "Want to talk to an old friend?"

Drollant smiled too, but feebly. He drew out his right hand, and Mago took it into his as he might have held a bird fallen from a tree.

"What's wrong? Where did the car hit you?"

Drollant seemed puzzled and lifted the sheet as if an inspection of his body would give him the answer. He gestured to Mago to look too.

"Well, your left leg's in a cast, *mon vieux*, and your chest is all strapped about with tape."

Up to now Drollant hadn't seen me at all. Mago was the most his horizon could hold. Now he did. "Cigarette?" he asked me, as if to be certain it really was.

"Yes," said Mago. "She brought me here and found you just where you are."

But Drollant wasn't much interested in me, and I decided this was the moment to leave them and try to find out how long Drollant would have to stay, that is if anybody would even so much as give me a decent "*bonjour*." So I told Mago where I was going and went to the head of the ward where a very starched woman at a desk was scribbling in an enormous book.

She glanced at me once and then ignored whatever flash of me she might have seen. I even tried a curtsy. I'd seen rich girls in the park duck down like that in front of

26

people they were meeting. That slid past her even faster, so I decided to try shock.

"Madame," I said in a calm voice, "may you be damned if you don't listen."

This she heard. "I will have you removed from the ward if you speak to me again," she hissed through her teeth.

I knew she meant it, but what was I to do? They might cart Drollant off any day now, and we'd never find him again. This would crack Mago right in his middle.

I had just raised my arm to bang on her desk when a little wren of a woman in a wrinkled blue uniform beckoned to me from the open door so violently that I obeyed and went over to her. She pulled me into the outer corridor.

"She's trouble," she began, pointing at Madame Starch. "You'd best leave her alone."

"I'd be happy to," I said, "but I have to find out something."

"What?"

"You work here?" I asked. I'd learned never to give out information free.

"Yes. I'm an aide. I clean up." She saw the doubt in my eyes. "But I know a lot, maybe even more than her."

Perhaps this tiny leftover from nowhere was crazy. Perhaps not. I'd give her a try. "See that boy leaning over the bed in the corner?"

My informant nodded.

"Well, his friend's got broken bones."

"And they take a long time to mend," she put in, guessing my next sentence. She waggled her head and continued. "So to ease the overcrowding they'll ship him

27

off to Pontmercy, probably in about two weeks. That's the usual period for bones."

"What's that—Pontmercy? Where is it?"

"About five hours from Paris by train. I know. I was there."

"You worked there?"

"No. I got beaten up by a mental patient. Both arms."

"What's it like?" I could have guessed but had to hear the facts. Mago would insist on them.

Her mouth, not much bigger than a raisin, twisted. "Hell," she said. "They mix them up, all kinds."

I now saw Mago coming toward the door, waving as he went at Drollant, who waved back.

"I want to thank you for your help," I said to the wren.

She smiled and then scurried off down the stairs.

After Mago and I were outside the building, I told him what I had learned.

He released a long whistle on one note. "It's obvious," he said, "what has to be done. We must extract Drollant from the hospital before they do."

"But how?"

"Money. We need money. Then we can put him in a cheap private clinic. There's one in our neighborhood. A good one, too. I know the man who delivers their vegetables."

I sighed. It was all right to talk about having to have money, but where in the universe could we get any?

We looked into each other's eyes, he into my green ones, me into his, searching for a lightning idea to hit us. It did. At just the same instant. Eel! I had said no to his plan for me to steal a painting from that artist—his name floated

28

back to me, Michel Courier—and sell it to the gallery owner, but did I any longer have the right to refuse?

Mago took my hand in his, and we walked very slowly and silently along the left quay of the Seine. We passed the bookstalls, all spilling over with books I'd never read. Maybe next time around. We even paused to watch two old men fishing. But the moment of speaking had to come, and when we were once more in our own room, its walls seeming somehow to be our protectors, I said the words Mago wanted to hear.

"I'll do it. Get Eel."

Five

MAGO DIDN'T HESITATE. He ran. While he was gone I lighted a small fire in the fireplace with sticks we had taken from the lumber yard downriver. I was suddenly cold. I shut out the crouching circle of thoughts that would have closed in on me and made the chills worse. I stared into the ribbons of flame until I seemed to become one myself, tall as a tower, flapping through the night until I scorched the moon.

I wasn't aware that the two of them had returned until Eel touched my hand. I'd rather it had been a toad.

"Now to business," he said immediately. "We've several strikes against us. You're young and unacquainted."

This roused me completely. "What does that mean?" I asked as haughtily as I could.

"You don't know much about the undersides of living. So you'll have to be carefully coached."

Mago must have sensed my resentment because he moved over close to me, his arm against mine. "She'll be fine," he said. "She's wholehearted."

I wished they would stop chewing over my character, but though I didn't know what Mago meant either, I was grateful for his support.

"We've got two weeks to raise the money, that right, Mago?"

"Less. Drollant has to be taken out of the hospital legitimately."

Eel smiled, making his mouth crooked on purpose. He had his own ideas about his attractiveness. "You think they're going to let a couple of underaged persons like you and Cigarette sign him out?"

"No," said Mago with his usual dignity. "My friend the laundry lady will do it for me."

"Okay," said Eel, somewhat miffed. "Now listen to my plan. Cigarette will make friends with the painter. Tomorrow at the latest. She has some charm and will use it on him so he is accustomed to her coming in and out of his loft. That way the theft will be easy. All she has to do is wait until he's out to dinner or something and then pinch the painting. Then you'll take it to Monsieur Flan at the gallery and get the money from him."

"But won't the painter know I took it?" I asked, the shivers in my spine now icy.

"Sure," responded Eel cheerfully. "You'll have to lie low for a while. Maybe get out of Paris."

I couldn't say another word. My whole life had in this instant become a pile of grimy crumbs to be ground under the first pair of shoes that came along.

I looked at Mago. He would save me if he could.

He couldn't. He was nodding his consent to Eel's plotting. It turned out they hadn't any definite plan as to how I was going to weasel myself into the painter's affections except to knock at his door and say I wanted to be a painter too someday. That would appeal to him, they said.

Well, they were right. That next morning, after I had washed my face and hands as dirtless as our arrangements allowed—the open spigot at the end of the alley and a thin triangle of soap that Drollant liked because it smelled of flowers, it was his treasure—I climbed the four flights to Michel Courier's studio, my heart beating in my ears louder than my footsteps.

He must have been just going out because the door swung open even before I could tap on it.

"Who are you?" he said, looking at me all over as if he were drawing me.

"I'd just like to see where you work, monsieur," I blurted, the rehearsed sentences about wanting to be a painter vanishing in my nervousness. I guessed now what Eel had meant when he said I was "unacquainted."

The man's eyebrows raised, but at the same time he smiled. "Come in then," he said. He stood back while I entered.

What a wonder it was! On the walls and leaning against them were houses and churches and men and children and trees and gardens and mountains and rivers and all kinds of skies and one very large snowstorm. I went round and round that long, light room, slower and slower, forgetting everything, even the man who had made what I was seeing. But when I came to the woman in green I had to halt.

As I kept looking at her deep green eyes, her hands that held a black cat, at the green softness of her dress, and herself as she rested against the trunk of a gray tree with red leaves, I knew this was the one I had to steal.

Not until I turned from her did I realize that the

painter had not said a word but had let me be free in his strange world.

Then I remembered why I was here. I tried to smile with some trace of dazzle but found I couldn't manage my mouth. It was tight to keep itself from trembling.

He spoke. "Why are you so moved?" he asked, and he came down to my level, sitting on his haunches.

His question was so natural, as though he had the right to ask it. I answered without thinking. "Because of all of these and this." I pointed toward the portrait.

"She is beautiful, isn't she? But you must have something of the eye of an artist yourself to recognize the work of a master."

I came all the way back to Drollant, Eel, and Mago. I had to. I was failing them fast.

I rummaged in the smallness of my brain for something that would begin the plan. "I am not an artist, monsieur," I said. "I don't even know what you put the paint on before you make a picture."

He smiled again. "That's simple. It's called a palette. Come over here and I'll show you."

He led me to what he named his easel. I'd never seen so many brushes all in one place, thin ones, bushy ones, blunt ones with very long handles. I liked the shape of what he called a palette. He let me hold it and put my thumb through the hole. I sniffed at the blobs of color.

Now he laughed. "That's oil and turpentine. You mix the paint with them. Want to try?"

"Oh, no! I'd just wreck the rainbow." I was looking back in my memory at the glass windows in the church.

"Then watch me for a moment," he said and dipped a

brush in a blue that was like midnight and gave three strokes to the half-filled oblong on the easel. They made part of a slate roof.

Once he started he couldn't seem to stop. I stood there, as intent as he was, for a time that couldn't be counted.

Finally he put down his brush and sagged into a cane chair. "I'm tired," he said as if to himself. "Too tired." Now he gazed at me without smiling, his eyes gone distant. "Would you like to pose for me? You would be interesting."

I was never sure what his "interesting" meant, not then or later, but it was my chance and I took it.

"Yes, please, monsieur. When?"

"Tomorrow morning at eight. I'll buy some rolls for us and heat up the coffeepot. I can't pay much, but maybe even that little will be of use to you."

I couldn't miss the echo of pity in his voice. I guess I must have looked like a waif to him in my stained pants and raveled sweater. So much the better, I said to myself, and then ran off down the stairs.

That evening, squatting in front of our hearth, the fire inside as meager as what we had just eaten, I recounted the meeting to Eel and Mago. Only I left out the good parts—how much I liked the picture of the woman, the man's kindness, and the colors.

Six

THE NEXT DAY and the next and the next were magically the same. I arrived at Monsieur Michel's loft at exactly eight, timed to the church bells in the neighborhood. He would shake my hand like I was a very welcome caller, not just somebody he'd hired to sit on a stool and be still while he sketched her. Then he'd pour me a mug of coffee with five lumps of sugar and hot milk and two soft rolls to dip into it, if I wished.

After such a good breakfast I could have sat all day, but at noon he locked up and went to a café for his lunch and then painted by himself the rest of the afternoon.

We didn't talk much together except once in a while about small and unimportant things. For instance, his studio had a skylight, and once I imagined it at night.

"Can you see the stars through the glass?" I asked.

"When I look," he said very seriously.

I understood. People didn't always look in the right places. I remembered once, when Mago and Drollant and I lived in the toolshed, waking up because I was cold, and I looked that night at Mago asleep. He was a second person, not someone I knew. His face was turned upward with a child's smiling, a child who had a home. I asked him the next morning what he had been dreaming, but he didn't know. There was nothing left over from that moment of joy.

Once when Michel had just finished painting a river with a bridge over it, I told him about Friquette. I think I told him because his river was so beautiful, with grass and willow trees at the edges. I wished Friquette's had been like it, not the Seine with its surface oil-stained from the barges and bits of trash floating around her as she went down.

He hadn't worked anymore that day and went to lunch early.

Then another time, when we were taking a break from work, Monsieur Michel started by saying, "I had a wife once."

"Like the lady in green?"

That startled him. "Yes. But how did you know?"

"I just knew," I answered. "Does she live in Paris?"

He shook his head sadly. "No. In the south, in a village named for a tree, a chestnut, Chataignier."

"Do you visit her often?"

"Only when I have to."

I knew he meant only when he got so lonely for her he couldn't stand it; and I knew, too, that she never sent for him. It would be the same between me and Mago if ever we had such a terrible quarrel he deserted me. Only with Michel it had been the other way around.

"Was the man who painted it a friend of yours, monsieur?" I didn't really want to know anything more about what I had bargained to take from him, but I could see he needed to talk about this person he so plainly loved.

"Of hers. She sat occasionally for special artists, and he was one. He gave it to her one year as a birthday present. She didn't want to take it, knowing how valuable his work was, but a refusal would have hurt his feelings."

"And when she left you, she gave it to you?"

"No. I asked for it." Michel's eyes were so distanced with sadness that I wished I were a sorceress and could magically bring his wife into the room, happy to be with him. "She knew why," he went on. "Because I couldn't bear to lose her entirely."

I clenched my hands, digging my fingernails into my palms until they stung. I wanted to vanish forever, disappear into nothingness before I had to force myself to take from this man the one thing most precious to him. But all I could do was to say I had a rendezvous with a friend and leave him.

Each morning he put me on a rickety stool and just drew whatever it was he saw of me. I stopped asking to see these sketches after the first few. They were too real.

"Am I really that dragged down?" I had said and grinned my best.

Monsieur Michel had laughed. "No, not always. Only when you are far away in your thoughts."

"Then I guess that's my natural face. Mago's got a word for it—doleful."

"Who's Mago?" he said, but rather absentmindedly as he charcoaled some more lines on his sheet of paper.

I knew immediately that mentioning Mago was a mistake. All the information Michel had about me was me alone. He mustn't ever connect the three of us.

"Oh, a person I met last week," I lied.

37

He continued to draw, and my worry evaporated.

That is, *that* worry did. The other loomed over those morning hours worse than a lumpy fear that had owned me ever since I was shoved into that second orphanage. Ghosts. I never talk about them. But what soiled the peace and the friendliness I had found in that loft was the almost-arrived day when I would have to destroy those mornings by stealing the lady in green.

Eel was getting impatient. The fourth evening he had acted very knifey, his voice sending splinters into my backbone. "It's got to be soon." He spoke only to Mago, never directly to me. "Want to set tomorrow?"

"That's for Cigarette to decide." Mago turned to where I was sitting, as apart from the two boys as I could get, trying to be more securely out of their conversation.

The silence was awkward. I simply shrugged. Suddenly the miserable supper of stale bread and cheese rinds, washed down by a single can of warm beer Mago had lifted from a woman's shopping basket, came up in my throat. How could I deprive Michel of his lady, the painting he could have sold for enough to give him a real studio in the best section of Paris, good clothes, and lots of treats for his comrades in any café he chose? If he kept her, refusing all these comforts, kept her out of love— how could I force myself to take her from him?

Mago seemed to sense at least part of what I was thinking. "We still have a few days' leeway," he said calmly to Eel. "No point in hassling Cigarette. She'll know when she can do it."

It was this touch of kindness that propelled me toward what I had agreed to do and what I so hated doing. And the next morning Monsieur Michel seemed almost to be cooperating, assisting me to carry out the loss of his precious painting.

He had just poured my coffee when I noticed he had added a special treat to our breakfast—two pastries. One was completely chocolate, seven paper-thin layers with cake between (I counted them) and the other a high ooze of whipped cream and raspberry jam.

Was he celebrating something?

"You choose first," he said, smiling.

How I would once have loved this delicious game! But now, with what was ahead of me, I wasn't at all sure I could even swallow any of this sweetness. I had a sudden glimpse of another kind of choice. Between two friends I had to select which one to betray, Mago or Michel. Not Mago, not ever. So it had to be the painter; and no matter how sickened I was with myself I had, now, to pretend to become the talking, acting imitation of goodness. I hoped my rottenness wouldn't show through.

"The chocolate, monsieur," I answered and instructed my mask to smile.

"I guessed as much," he said, pleased, and placed the cake in front of me on a scrap of discarded paper.

I stared at the brown square and saw that it rested on a rough sketch of myself, one eye staring back at me from under the edge. With a forefinger dipped in the icing I smudged the eye out.

"You're probably wondering why the extravagance," the artist commented, glancing a little ruefully at the cracked walls and shabby furnishings of his studio.

But I could tell he was very happy about something. How I wished I were the same person I was before Drollant's accident, before the adoption of Eel's plan.

Then I could have helped Michel make this into a party. We might have sung a song together or invented nonsense.

All I could manage was, "I did wonder why."

"I'm going south," he said.

This meant nothing to me until I saw him turn around and look at the lady in green.

"To see your wife?"

"Yes. She doesn't know it. I'm just going."

"When will you be back?" The thief in me had to know. The other self wanted to shorten the separation by being given a time limit. I couldn't, right then, imagine not ever seeing him again.

His expression was anxious with a light of hope. "I don't know. Maybe in a week, maybe never. But you're not eating." He had gulped his pastry down in three bites.

I'd never had to force food down my throat ever in my life before. Now I had to and I did. I could feel the chocolate lump in my stomach.

"It depends on her, doesn't it, monsieur?" There was nothing bold in my question, just caring.

He showed no surprise and went on talking. "Yes. When we were married—she'd never had anything to do with anyone like me before, somebody who had to paint, no matter what—she liked our life at first. She owned a house here in Paris and built me a studio in the rear garden, and all my friends—they were many then—came to see us, and every night was like a party." He paused as if the past had momentarily become the present for him.

"And you painted all day in your little house?" I prompted. His confiding his story to me was so painful my bones began to ache.

"Yes. Then one morning she said she was leaving. For good."

"Did she tell you why?" This was the lady in the painting, an image so tender that just looking at her I had felt her love. Surely she could never have been cold or cruel to this man who was himself so kind.

"Yes. She said she had been too lonely."

"But you were there with her."

"Not truly," he murmured, and he got up and went to the windows. His next words I sensed were his last. "And I never knew what I had lost until she left."

I stood up too, scrumpled the improvised cake plates into a ball, and threw them in the barrel that was his waste basket. I saw now the little pile of belongings beside the door, a backpack and a bedroll.

"I see you're ready," was all I could think of to say. A tiny root of hope curled into my brain. Maybe he would make it impossible for me to get back into the loft after he had gone. Maybe I could return to Mago and Eel with an excuse that would shield me from what I had agreed to do.

But as Michel hoisted the pack onto his back and shouldered the bedroll he said the one thing that kept me a captive of the plot. "I've paid the rent for two months ahead, so the place remains mine for that long. If I don't come back before then, the landlady has agreed to give safe storage to my few possessions until I can arrange to collect them. I'm going to leave the key where you'll know where to find it and return it to her. Perhaps you could look in from time to time and help with the moving, if it comes to that. Will you do me this favor? I know I can rely on you."

Now the ache inside me changed to a stab in my ribs. I could only nod and watch as he fitted the key into a crack in the wooden molding that lined the floor in the hall.

He said goodbye in the street by kissing me on both cheeks twice over and then strode away and out of sight.

I shut my eyes tight and stayed blind for a long time.

Seven

THE NEXT DAWN was one I didn't want to wake up to, but I did, many times before true daylight. I had skimmed sleep all night. The gold and orange of the sky as I exited into the street seemed a kind of reproach, and I walked to the studio with my head down, seeing only the stained cobblestones and the uneven curbing. I was alert enough to what I was doing, however, to take a complete look around before I entered the hallway of Monsieur Michel's building. The only person up and about was an old man sweeping a stoop two blocks away, and he was staring at his broom.

I tiptoed the three flights so lightly that even I couldn't hear my footsteps. There were no sounds from behind the many doors I passed. My legs felt as though they were dragging chains.

At last my fingers were picking the key from its hiding place, and I held my breath as I fitted it into the lock. I could still choose not to turn it, not to open that door on a life that would forever after be filled with fear and shame. But I knew I had to. For Mago. If I let him down, I was nobody.

A thin streak of light touched the painting like a long,

ghostly arm directing me. I hurriedly took it down from the wall, wrapped it any which way in some newspapers piled in a corner of the loft, and let myself out, carefully replacing the key.

I was holding the frame so tightly that one of the corners dug into my armpit, but I was afraid that if I shifted it, I might simply let it drop and run away.

I got as far as the last landing when a door opened right in front of me and a huge woman shoved herself against my body. Her worn, grease-splotched robe caught on one edge of the frame. She jerked it free.

"Damn nuisances, you children!" she almost spat at me. "Always cluttering up the halls. Shouldn't be allowed."

I waited, absolutely still.

"Can't even go to the toilet without bumping into one of you!"

I don't think she even saw me, at least not clearly, out of those small, blurred eyes. She lumbered to the end of the corridor, slamming herself shut behind the door marked with WC.

After that I raced to the alley just behind the gallery and gagged with the relief of finding Mago in the shelter of a fire escape, expecting me.

I handed him the painting. He knocked on the rear door of the gallery where the owner lived.

In two minutes Monsieur Flan opened it just wide enough to view his visitor through a crack.

"What do you want?" he asked in a voice like someone blowing through a grass blade.

"I have what you want," was Mago's reply.

"And that is?" he squeaked.

"Let me in and I'll show you."

Glimpsing the shape of what Mago carried, Monsieur Flan came into full sight. He gestured Mago into the back room, not quite closing the door. I could hear every word that passed between them, and even if I hadn't, I would have waited to see Mago safely outside.

First I heard the fall of the newspaper, then a gasped "*Mon Dieu!*" followed by a very brief silence.

"You stole it, of course," came the pinched voice of the art dealer.

"No, monsieur," seemed to rise from Mago's stomach it was so low-pitched.

"Don't talk nonsense. But it's of no importance to me how you procured it. It will have to be sold through secret channels, in any case, where no one will investigate the provenance."

"Provenance?" asked Mago.

I jigged up and down, not from the cold but from impatience because I wanted him to get done with the whole miserable affair as fast as it would take Monsieur Flan to take out his wallet and hand over the money. I had a terrible feeling that a giant spider was winding his web around Mago only he didn't know it.

"A proof of where it came from. But enough of that. I will give you fifteen thousand francs, no more, no less." He didn't wait for Mago's answer but went on. "Naturally, you will maintain complete silence as to this transaction. If not, you will find yourself in dire trouble. I will see to it."

"Agreed."

"Now go. I will look forward to never seeing you again." There was a high kind of chittering in his tones, like a rat suddenly surrounded by a wall of cheese.

Mago came out of the doorway so fast he must have

been shoved. "Cigarette!" he exclaimed. "I told you to be careful. Hanging around here only increases the risks."

"I'm sorry, Mago," I told him, keeping my voice very quiet. "But I had to know how everything turned out."

He looked into my eyes as though he could see my thoughts in them. Then he smiled. "I understand," was all he said, but it was enough.

I went with him to Madame Laurier's laundry and stood in his shadow as he talked to the tall, bony woman whose gray eyes gleamed like pebbles under water.

I admired how Mago eased this severe woman into a sort of softness as he told her about Drollant, the accident, and why he must be saved from being sent to an institution.

She protested this at first. "He'd get regular meals and a bed better than I'm certain you can provide."

"Yes," Mago agreed, "but what he needs most is someone who cares about him. He goes to pieces very quickly, and when that happens he's all alone unless I'm there. We will take him to a clinic."

We both waited, watching for a sign either of refusal or consent, and when it came it was so surprising that Mago almost ducked. This stiff woman, who seemed as unhuman as her ironing board, raised both her rough hands and cupped Mago's face. "I will do it," was all she said.

When she changed out of her work clothes and was buttoning her black coat up to her neck, she spoke again. "I must be paid, you know, for my lies."

Mago nodded. "How much?"

What she asked amounted to a third of the money Monsieur Flan had given us, but Mago's cheerfulness didn't lessen. "When he is safely out of the hospital, I will give you your money."

She threw him a glance that held respect and strode several steps ahead of us all the way to the city hospital. Once inside the reception hall there was no hesitation about her; she acted as though she managed the place. I don't think anyone, from the man on duty downstairs to the head nurse in Drollant's ward, even noticed how rubbed with wear her coat was down the sides or that the heels of her shoes were so crooked that they made her feet turn outward. They were too impressed by the strength of her demand that Drollant be released immediately in her charge. They never even asked for proof that she was his aunt. She even almost convinced me that she was, just for that moment.

I got a glimpse of the little gray person who had helped me before with the information that Drollant was to be shipped off. She smiled at me as a nurse heaved Drollant into a wheelchair and pushed him to the elevators, Madame Laurier and Mago walking beside with me in the rear.

The laundress didn't smile, but she gave me a wink. I wished I could have bought her a bunch of white and red roses. I don't know why roses except they seemed proud enough to match what she was doing.

Drollant just sat huddled over himself until we were outside and into a taxi. He was propped between Mago and me. He was so absent I wondered if maybe he didn't recognize us. Then Mago covered one of Drollant's hands with his own. Drollant turned his head and stared down at it. Then his gaze traveled along Mago's arm, up to his shoulder, and finally reached his eyes.

47

What he was searching for he found. Suddenly his pinched face bloomed to such a smiling that Mago burst into laughter and squeezed him tight in an enormous hug.

From then on there was no stopping the chatter that came out of our invalid. It lasted until the cab drew up to the entrance of the clinic. Drollant could tell it wasn't an ordinary house, especially when Madame Laurier vanished inside and reappeared with a nurse and another wheelchair. He clamped on to Mago's arm so hard that Mago winced.

"This isn't like the last place," Mago began whispering in his ear. "They like you here. You'll see for yourself in just a minute. Trust me."

I hoped, as we walked in, that it wouldn't be all white with bare walls. It wasn't. The pale green against the white woodwork went with the soft beige chairs and shiny tables. I guessed that those got polished every morning.

Mago transferred Drollant's grip to my arm. "You stay here with Cigarette while Madame Laurier and I make the arrangements. All right?"

Drollant nodded, but he was still wary, so I began to point out to him the pictures on the walls. They were all five of gardens filled with what seemed to me rather mushy flowers except for one. I momentarily forgot Drollant as I watched how tall trees grew on each side of a dusty road, how the grass seemed to have pushed up between them—not from the painter's brush but truly. I could almost feel the sun of that picture touching my own cheeks.

Drollant was tugging at me now. "Cigarette," he said, "where were you?"

I was about to tell him when Mago, Madame Laurier,

48

and a man in a dark brown suit came out of another room. The man was nodding agreeably, and I was astonished to see him pat Mago's head.

"Quite a little man of affairs, is he not, madame?" he was saying.

"Oh, yes, indeed," said Madame Laurier, her smile a little forced. "He is a good son to me and understands my finances better than I do."

The brown man shook hands all around. "Well, I am certain the young one will be happy here." He crooked his finger at a nurse standing near. "Mademoiselle Fenel will take him to his room and introduce him to the other children."

I didn't go up in the elevator with Mago and Drollant and their guide but waited with Madame Laurier in the reception hall. She was sort of chuckling to herself as she murmured, "Never heard anything like it in my life the way that boy maneuvered me into being his mother with Drollant his younger brother."

Mago didn't take long, and there was a satisfied look about him until he saw me. Then he frowned.

"Madame Laurier," he said, "you know how grateful I am for your assistance." He slipped the money into the pocket of her coat. "I think you will find the amount exact."

We followed him out of the clinic. As we reentered the world of streets and strangers Mago took on an alertness that I began to feel inside myself.

He held out his hand to the laundry lady as though dismissing her.

With a "Thank you and I'll see you soon again, children," she left us.

"Now." He gripped me by the shoulders. "You must take off immediately—leave Paris. No telling when the painter will come back."

"Where will I go?" I couldn't imagine myself without Mago.

"To a town. Get a job, any kind, so you'll seem to belong there."

"But how will you know where I am?"

"You will send Drollant a postcard. We will join you just as soon as he is on his feet again." He drew from a pocket a little cloth bag tied at the top with string. It was stuffed full.

"Here. There's enough money in this to keep you, if you're careful, until we get together again."

"How about you?" I rummaged for words, any words, to delay his going. "You've been handing out francs in fistfuls to everyone else."

He smiled at this. "Dear little sparrow. You must learn not to worry about the people you love." He held me very close to him and then with two quick kisses on my cheeks he left me.

Eight

I WENT BLANK FOR A WHILE. I could see where I was going, crossed the streets when the avalanche of cars stopped for the traffic lights, and didn't bump into anybody; but I just wasn't there, inside myself. Mago had taken me with him, and the body that was walking over the bridge and into a park looked like me but was really a hollowness with the wind blowing through its bones.

I must have gone a long way because when I came to, standing in front of the great, windowed building where Mago had taken the flowers for Friquette, my legs were aching so hard I went in through the high doors to find a place to sit down.

I went directly to Mago's lady. The rack at her feet was filled with candles. Their little fires seemed to flicker a kind of warmth down to me, though I still couldn't feel my toes. I looked upward, expecting the colored glass to shine on me, but the radiance I remembered had gone from them. Maybe it was just for that moment and never again. So I stopped searching for those same reds and blues and greens and returned to the lady.

She had no comfort for me. For Mago that far-ago day, but not now for me. Her eyes were shadowed, and I saw a wide crack across the hand that was reaching out. It was made of wood, and the wood had split.

Then a strange thought stained my mind. Maybe she, like me, was a betrayer. Maybe she made promises she didn't keep. Maybe she gathered up all those things people asked of her and threw them into a sewer hole, the way I had thrown Monsieur Michel's gift of trust and affection down on the ground and stamped on it.

An anger rose in me that burned as truly as if I had held my arms over the candle flames until the skin blackened. For an instant I wanted to push the lady off her stand, to beat my fists against her wooden face. But then, as suddenly, I knew it was myself I wanted to pound, to bruise, to hurt over and over again.

I was no better than that rag of a person Mago had found sniveling in the basement of the orphanage. I was worse. I had made the choice to be a thief and a deceiver and could blame no one but myself.

I left the lady and her vast house crying, crying for what I no longer was.

I was no sooner outside, trying to wipe off the tears before the wind did, than I was slammed flat against a wall and held there. The stones iced my back, but what I saw in front of me was worse. There stood Eel, so close I had to turn my head away from the sourness of his breath.

"Got you!" he was saying. "Hung around so long I thought you'd joined the church. What's in there for you anyway?"

When I began to struggle to free my arms from the terrible pinching of his hands, he kicked my shin. The pain stilled me. "What do you want?" I gritted through my clenched teeth.

He laughed in a high, false cackle. "What do you think, little innocent?" He thrust one hand into my jacket pocket and drew out the wad of francs Mago had given me. "Is this all of it?" He touched my face with his fist.

I nodded. What I cared about in that moment was to escape his awfulness.

He barred me across the neck with one arm while he riffled through the bills. "Looks like he gave you most of his share, too. Well, that's what I call Eel's luck. Never ask, just take." He grinned down at me, his mouth a sliver of derison. "Learn that from me, Cigarette. Learn it good. Maybe someday you'll thank old Eel. Mago could use a little of my schooling too."

He withdrew his arm. My body was free, but I wasn't.

"What do you mean?" I asked, moving out of his reach.

"About Mago? Thought that would interest you. From now on he is going to work for me."

"He won't! I know he won't!"

"No? What a stupid little scut you are, no more sense than a rabbit. If he doesn't, I'll turn him in to the police. You don't imagine, do you, I was ordering a seven-course lunch while you and he were in the alley exchanging the painting, or that I wasn't a witness to his coming out of Flan's back door without it? That's all the police need to know to pull him in and lock him up until he's old enough to grow a beard."

I wished I had a knife. I would have slashed that leering face to shreds just to shut him up. I had never in my whole life before wanted to destroy anybody. My fingers became claws, and I raised my hands to scratch his face bloody. But he danced off down the street and around the corner before I could strike him.

As abruptly as my arms dropped to my sides I knew what I had to do next. I hadn't realized that I had placed Mago in danger. I must find Monsieur Michel. Only he could claim the painting as his, and if getting it back meant turning me in as the one who stole it—well, that was what I deserved. Mago had to be kept free of bondage to the terrible Eel. His life would become a misery. As to mine? I think, if I could have, I would have buried myself in the dirt of the nearest park, smothered up my mouth with dead leaves so that no words would ever come out of it again.

But tomorrow would not allow such a choice, or even the many tomorrows ahead of me. The first thing was to find a map of France. I remembered seeing one displayed in the window of a bookshop somewhere near the flower market, and after choosing six wrong streets, I finally found it. The map was still there, stretched between two piles of leather-bound books. But as I gazed at it my heart lurched. I couldn't read well enough.

I shuttered my eyes with my hands, exhausted by this last blow. I was idiot enough to pray that when I opened them again a miracle would have inserted itself in my brain and the letters on the map would tell me something. No miracle but the wedge of one. I had learned the abc's and a few simple words. Could I piece them together, the letters of the place Monsieur Michel had mentioned? *Chataignier*. I said the whole alphabet out loud and paused at the *s*. Then I began to scan the map. The search was so hopeless that I almost abandoned it.

Then, as though flashed on an inner screen, the word *chat*, "cat," appeared in my head. *Chat. Chataignier.* Tracing my finger down the glass, southward, the map behind, I had it in two minutes.

I memorized as best I could the route leading from Paris. But the network of roads, once in the country, was too complicated to fix in my mind. I would have to depend on asking later on. I wondered how far it was from town to town, because the route was a lot of little squiggles pieced together from Paris to the south. Would I ever get there now that Eel had stolen any chance of taking trains and buses?

But, most of all, how would I ever get anywhere without Mago? Like suddenly discovering there were wings attached to my shoulder blades, one thought gave me flight from my worries: maybe Mago would go with me! A whisper inside me warned against any such rise of hope, but for a few hours at least, I had a way to follow.

I had to wait for night in case the police were looking for me around Mago's building. I spent those long hours in whatever shelters welcomed someone like me: doorways, a department store, the entrances to the Metro; and once, when the chill was like nettles on my skin, I tried a café where people in old clothes were hunched over coffee or a bowl of soup. But the proprietor put me out before I'd even had time to warm my breath. And the tireder I got, the more distant was the vision of me and Mago together on the road to Chataignier.

At last the sky darkened and I dared to creep up the stairs to our living place. The doorknob clicked as I turned it so that I met a startled Mago as I slipped inside. He was sitting before the fireplace.

"What are you doing here, Cigarette?" His question was

55

tense, a little angry. "I had imagined you safe away by now."

"I had to come," I said, stammering slightly from the shock of his disapproval.

"Why? You may be picked up. Someone in the neighborhood might have seen you with the painting."

"It's Eel. He's going to make a slave of you."

"That's nonsense. You made it up."

"I didn't! He told me himself!"

Mago turned away from me so that I couldn't see his face, but his voice came thickly from his throat when he next spoke. I half imagined he was stifling tears.

"Oh, Little Cigarette," he said, "you must begin to think of yourself first. It's the only way people like you and me can survive."

A kind of bleak happiness returned to me. He was teaching me something again, like before. I couldn't help it. I ran to him and clung to his back, my arms around his neck, my face pressed to him so tightly that I could feel the ridge of his spine. "Come with me," I said.

He let me hold on to him for a very long moment, then gently shrugged me off. "I can't come with you. I must stay near Drollant until he can travel." He sat me down in front of him, and it might have been that first day in the basement of the orphanage. "Now I want you to listen," he said.

I had always listened to Mago, but now every word was prized.

"You are to say to yourself, as many times as it takes to know it is true, 'I am Cigarette. I am real, myself, and someone to honor.' Say it."

I said it, but the words sounded in my ears like parrot talk.

"That's not very good," he said, "but it's a beginning. Promise me that whenever you find yourself without courage, you will repeat it."

I promised. The sentence, just because he had given it to me, would be a sort of guard against despair.

He got up and spread a stack of sacks to make a bed for me. "Sleep now, but you must be gone before daybreak."

Then his solemnity broke and he grinned. "Forgot to invite you to my feast." He drew out a chain of small sausages and a loaf of bread from the box that was our cupboard and placed them on a newspaper. "Would you like to prepare it?" From behind the box he brought out a half-bottle of wine.

When we had drunk a glassful apiece, we were able to laugh. Later, when I was tucked under the rough covers of my bed, I ducked into dreaming to avoid the morning to come.

Nine❦

THE NEXT MORNING was no morning at all. A pall of grayness had overtaken the sky, the buildings, the cobbled streets. This dulled color seemed to predict a kind of hopelessness that was so strong in me I had to waken Mago. Oh, I knew he would rather I just slipped out, leaving last night a brighter goodbye, but I couldn't. I needed at least a few more moments with him to hang on to.

I poked him very gently on the tip of his chin. The touch must have reminded him of something he liked because his eyes opened and his mouth smiled in the very same instant.

He sat up. "It had to be you or a mouse," he said, making me smile too. "But to business. Ready to go? Your money snugged away in a safe place?"

I nodded rather than commit a spoken lie. He would have given me part of his share, and I knew Drollant needed it. "And I know where I'm heading."

Mago's smile became a grin. "That's my Cigarette. Where?"

"A town called Chataignier. It's in the south. They have a factory there which employs children my age and no questions asked." I had to invent something. I wasn't going to reveal my plan to get Monsieur Michel to reclaim the painting so that Mago could get out from under the bondage of Eel. Mago might forbid it, and if he did, I would have to obey.

"We'll find it, Drollant and me. No use now to send a postcard. We'll just come."

He stood up, and I recognized a finality. I was to go now.

I threw myself against him so hard that I could hear his breath huff out. My right ear, pressed on his chest, listened to five beats of his heart before he withdrew from me, and capping my shoulders with both hands, he turned me toward the doorway.

I fled into the refuge of the street, welcoming the stench of the drains, the heavy dampness of the air. I headed for the nearest train station. Maybe I could sneak onto one of the carriages. I wanted to get out of Paris as fast as I could to ease the loss of Mago. Maybe the new strangeness of houses and people would help to overlay the pain inside me.

Except for the carts of mail sacks waiting to be loaded and a scatter of country people, their cardboard suitcases roped closed, the train platforms were empty. I knew I would appear too conspicuous among them, a small girl without a surrounding family, so I placed myself beside a station master, keeping alert to the first sign of any departure.

The man seemed to be studying me as we stood together, and I was about to move off when he spoke. "I wouldn't try it if I were you. Just give yourself trouble."

"Try what?" I asked, bold as I could.

I must not have been very successful because he laughed. "You little sparrows amuse me. You hop about the streets of the city picking up what you can, going from here to there. If you ever flew away, I'd miss you." He straightened his cap and stopped smiling. "But I'm bound to warn you that no one rides free on my trains."

I liked this man. Maybe because he liked me. So I was frank with him. "Then how am I going to travel south?" I asked him.

For some reason, this brought outright laughter. When he had finished, he drew out a white handkerchief, blew his nose like a trumpet, folded the square, and returned it neatly to his pocket. Then, as if making an official announcement, he said, "You will go with my cousin Jean who is trucking some storage to Tours this afternoon. I'll take you to his apartment right after you and I have our lunch."

I couldn't really respond to his goodness. I was too surprised. But as I waited for the station clock to strike noon I wondered about a lot of things, one among them if maybe the spirit of Mago was with me, seeing that I met this kind man who understood without being told. And, a little later, when I was sitting at his table, eating sausages and spinach, I was sure of it. His cousin had immediately consented to take me as far as he was going and even suggested that I pack an extra sweater as the nights were cold in the country.

I didn't mention that all my extras were invisible, but when he went to get his truck from the garage, the station master disappeared for a few moments and came back with a cardboard box tied around with string. "Here, take this. I put in a pair of wool socks—a few sizes too large, to be sure, but warm—and a scarf I don't need any longer. It all gives the appearance of luggage."

I was grateful, but I didn't know how to show it other than to offer him my hand. He shook it with ceremony. In five minutes I was seated beside his cousin in the cab of his truck.

I had never ridden in a truck before, and I enjoyed the roar of the motor starting up and the feeling of being above everyone in the street, perched really like a sparrow on the high seat.

The cousin wasn't very talkative. In fact, he never said anything until we reached the outskirts of Paris and then only to tell me that the route might be bumpy and that I could hold on to the door handle if I wished. I didn't mind his silence. It left me free to watch the slums move backward and make way for the villages. He honked through their narrow streets, warning children and chickens that the monster was coming, and for a while I pretended that I was riding the neck of a dragon, his fires streaking on both sides of me like rockets. I'd have to remember to tell Mago about all this. He liked the telling of things.

As though he had caught the tail of my thought, the cousin spoke. "Would you sing me a song?" he asked as he rubbed his eyes. "I'm slightly sleepy, and it would help to clear my mind."

He didn't know how hard was the task he gave me. I heard again the strong sending of Mago's voice as he sang that day he taught me to be pitiful, and I had to scrape my throat clear of waiting tears. But I did it. I sang his song.

61

I'll tell you a river
I'll tell you a tree
If you give me a sliver
Of charity.

I'll bring you a fish
Of silver and gold
A leaf like a wish
Before I'm old.

I'll gather a flower
To match your eyes
I'll find you a flutist
Just my size.

Give me a ring
To buy my bread
And I'll crown you a king
Before I'm dead.

I'll give you as true
As the sky above
If you give me a sou
I'll give you love.

There was a small silence between us when I had finished. Then the cousin merely said, "That's a sad song."

"But it is full of promises." Mago wasn't a sad person, not even when the worst of winter bit into him.

"And no way to keep them," he commented.

I kept quiet after that until we rattled onto the cobblestones of a large town. "Where are we?" I asked.

"Tours. I'll be stopping here for about an hour to take on a load. Then I go back."

I explained that my journey was southward, and thanking him I called out goodbye as I rounded the first corner.

The night was already half arrived. When I saw ahead an open gate that led into a wide courtyard, I turned in, hoping to find a niche somewhere for sleeping in. The enormous tree that centered the semicircle of cream-colored buildings would have been shelter enough in the summer, but already the coldness that came with the dark was coating my arms and legs. I took the scarf from the box the station master had given me and wrapped it twice around my neck, then pulled up the wool socks over my own shoes. I stashed the box under the tree, and at that moment I saw the stall. This would do. I squeezed myself between one wall of the inside and something round and gray. I looked up. It was an elephant—a life-sized stuffed elephant. *

I reached up and patted his dusty trunk. Between his feet was a plaque, but I couldn't read it. Somehow, suddenly, it seemed as though Mago had directed me to this strange companion. How he would laugh when I told him about it! Just thinking of his amusement made me laugh, and I must have gone to sleep smiling because as though no more than a minute had passed I opened my eyes and it was morning.

I got up and greeted my friend, the elephant, who answered back as well as he could from behind the dulled

*In 1906 an elephant named Fritz died in Tours while traveling with the Barnum & Bailey Circus. His stuffed remains were given by the circus to the children of the town, who often bring him offerings of flowers.

glass of his eyes. I folded the socks over my belt, and leaving the courtyard, turned away from where I had come the night before. One block farther on I halted in front of another of the lady's houses, only this time the church was smaller. I recognized it as hers by the arched doorways and all the little stone people sitting on top of one another in columns. Maybe Mago would like it if I went in and said "*bonjour*" to her. So I did.

Thin rays of early sunlight, like long straws, shone through the windows. I walked across their reds and blues and purples wishing their colors would dye me all over speckled so that I'd never lose their brightness.

Two old women, dressed in black, were murmuring to themselves up front where the lady was; only this statue was clothed in brown instead of blue. But she did look just like Mago's friend. I sat down in a row of little chairs and propped my elbows on the odd half-table in front of me. I was hungry, but there was no use asking the lady for anything. I didn't have Mago's connection with her.

And then I saw it—a string bag just a yard away filled with bread, onions, cheese, and three apples. Nobody was beside it. I hastily tucked it under my chair and tiptoed up to the railing that kept anyone from touching the lady. Being careful not to catch the attention of the two women, I whispered my thanks. I got no response from her, though she was gazing down in my direction with a lot of sweetness in her face, but if Mago believed she could hear, then she could.

I hurried back to my sack and left her house, already munching one of the apples.

I decided to walk the cold out of my legs and within a

few minutes came to the bridge that led across the river and to the south. I paused to watch the slow drift of the shallow water passing the tiny islets of sand and bushes. I wondered what it would be like to live on one of them with a little boat for company and brief journeys downriver, but always safe and private.

The rumbling of a bus broke into my daydream, and I trotted the rest of the way to the far bank. I turned off the main road and took a narrower one edged by a canal and what seemed to be an endless row of poplar trees.

I had walked for an hour and was beginning to doubt my having chosen a country road when I was halted so abruptly by what I saw that I almost stumbled. To my right, at the end of a double line of giant elms, rose, white and majestic, my first castle. It had to be one. There were walled gardens, a small tower leading on to a drawbridge, and surrounding the tall, four-towered building, a moat with swans. But, most beautiful of all, the castle spanned the river, arch after arch.

Like someone gone suddenly stupid, I let my feet take me to the entrance. A fat woman jostled me awake, and I realized that I was surrounded by visitors, all waiting to go inside. I had to go with them. I had to see what the outside promised. After one look at the portly height of the guide, I knew I could never sneak past him.

At that instant I saw a little girl quietly chewing on a stiff, pink piece of paper that must be a ticket. Her family was taking photographs and had their backs to the child. Quick as a bird after a worm, I snatched the ticket from her and ducked toward the front of the group. She howled her anger, but she was too young to explain and got a slap for her carelessness. I was somewhat sorry about that, but I soon forgot her as we passed across the planked bridge and into the main hall of the castle.

The sweep of the curved stone staircase with leaves carved into the banister stopped my breath. Then I saw the black and white squares of the floor, the high, pointed doorways leading into a room filled with old wooden chests and chairs and a fireplace so deep I could have skipped rope in it. I felt like floating. As we went from one great room to the next I kept my arms close to my sides because if I had lifted them, even an inch, I might have risen into the air.

The next room was the last. A long expanse shimmering with mirrors, with the reflections on the ceiling of the silver flow of the river beneath. I guess I lost myself then because the next thing I knew the guardian was shoving me from behind, saying that the visit was over and that no lingering was allowed.

I don't know where the afternoon went. I continued on down the road. I ate my bread and cheese with an onion between, and I must have passed trees and flowers and houses and maybe even people, but I was still in my castle. Only the descent of dusk woke me at last. I knew I must find a place to spend the night.

It must have been close to midnight before I saw the glint of a lamp in the window of what seemed to be more a shack than a house. The moonlight wavered through the trees that shrouded it as though reluctant to touch it, and my thoughts were wavering too. I was very tired. I needed a place, any place, to lie down. Maybe that was why the person who came to open her door to me didn't disgust me.

66

She was so filthy that her skin was crusted over brown, her wrinkles like cracks in dried mud, and the smell of her was worse than rotted garbage. But she beckoned me in, and right then I was too exhausted to care. She offered me a bowl of what might have been potato soup, but I saw something floating just beneath the surface that wasn't a vegetable, and I shook my head, trying to smile.

So far there had been no words between us, but now she spoke. "I've a nice little loft just up that ladder, and the mattress has a warm quilt on it. Go up and sleep, little one; sleep well."

I had no choice. It was either her loft or collapsing slowly into a faint. I pulled myself up the ladder and fell like a stone onto the bed.

I think it must have been the cry of a bird or an animal that woke me a few hours later. There was a desperation in the sound that quickened me to sit up and then to stand, listening. There was no repetition of that despair.

I peeked over the edge of the loft, and what I saw dug at my stomach. She held a wooden doll in her left hand and was bashing its head against the floor. I may have screamed as I scudded down the rungs of the ladder. I don't know. But what I did know was the vicious blow on the side of my head from her hard and scabby right hand. I staggered, half falling. The room blurred around me.

She cackled like a hen. "That'll teach you to mind." Her voice was hideously pleased. "I've always wanted a pet," she said. "And you can also be useful."

I tried to blank my imagination as to what uses she might put me and glared at her so she wouldn't see my fear.

She glared back, but in a rather pleased way, as though

she and I were joined in a kind of grim game. "Need more firewood," she said. "Won't be long."

When the door had slammed after her, I frantically rattled the doorknob. Locked.

There was a crack and a thump from the forest as though my captor was stepping on underbrush. The sound seemed to come nearer every second. I bit my lips to keep from crying out.

The door opened and there she stood, blocking the entrance, her arms filled with short branches.

I knew I had only one chance. I took it. I shoved the load from underneath, and the sticks flew into her face.

I dashed forward. She lurched to one side, and as I passed her she ripped the length of my right arm with her jagged fingernails.

But nothing, not even a pack of wild dogs, could have stopped the force of my going. I ran until my ribs hurt and finally slowed to a walk because I had to.

How welcome that dusty road, that dawn sky! How sweet the smell of the grass that walled the borders!

I was hungry, my bag of food left behind. My arm was burning. But I was grateful for all that. I was free.

I walked a long while, with only apple trees for company. Then, just ahead, I saw a square, white building with a bell on top of it. The ground around it was packed hard as though many people had trampled on it for a long time. I crossed over to the miniature porch. I tried the handle of the door. It opened.

I was in one of the strangest rooms I'd ever seen. Long benches with equally long tables in front of them striped the whole of the space except for an oblong table at the front, facing the benches. Back of this table was a slate board as black as tar. This must be a school. We had had one at the orphanage, but it was not like this; and the youngest children, like me, had sat on the floor. There had been no slate board.

Then I saw the chalk box. I touched each color with my forefinger, and when I came to the purple I rubbed a smear of it on the slate. I was reminded of those first glass windows. Without thinking of anything except that here was my first chance to put one color beside another, taking the blue, the yellow, and the green in my left hand I began to draw a hill with the purple. The hurting from the burn was soon forgotten as a forest of trees appeared in front of the hill and then a meadow of grass and flowers.

I don't know how long I stood there, adding shape after shape—a house, two rather awkward horses, and a girl in the garden reaching for a rose.

Three words in a voice like the purple chalk stopped me. "Who are you?"

I turned, so startled I dropped the handful of colors. They rattled onto the floor.

Just inside the doorway was the thinnest woman I had ever seen, but somehow her thinness made her beautiful. Her face was long and all bones, her eyes so deeply socketed that they were mysterious. And there was nothing threatening in the tone of her voice.

"I just came in," I stammered.

"Then stay awhile," she said, and now the bell was ringing.

A stampede of children poured in and took their places at the tables. Each one had a stack of books. They stared at me as though I were a monkey or a homeless dog.

The woman moved to the front and seated herself

behind her table. "We have a visitor today, children," she said and inclined her head toward me. "An artist. Helene, please let her have your place for the morning."

A girl who had been criticizing my worn clothes and cracked shoes with eyes like bits of mica in the pavements of Paris obeyed, and I sat down hard on that bench just to get partly out of sight. I could feel my face as hot as the burn on my arm.

"I will not erase this very talented mural until tomorrow," the narrow woman was saying, "so that we can continue to enjoy it." She glanced at me and then opened one of her books and the lessons began.

It was not until the sun was well up and the morning almost gone that she dismissed the class for what she called a "recess." She gestured to me to stay where I was. When the room was empty, she came to sit beside me.

"Now we can talk," she said and leaned toward me. "But you are badly cut, child! You must have something to put on it." She drew a key from her handbag. "My house is just at the first crossroads from here, painted green with two pine trees at the gate. I want you to let yourself in, and on the kitchen shelf above the sink is a bottle of antiseptic. Put it on liberally and wait for me. I go home for lunch. We will have it together."

What kind of a person was this, I wondered, to trust me with free entry to her house? I might put fire to it or steal her jewels or break the windows just for meanness. Eel would have. How did she know I wouldn't?

She may have guessed my thoughts because she put her arm around my shoulders and said, "Go quickly now. You'll be much more comfortable when you've taken care

70

of that wound." She practically ushered me out of the building and watched as I went down the road. The second time I looked back she waved.

I did as I was told, and she was right. That yellow stuff stung, but some of the redness went. I inspected her provisions and fixed a kind of meal for the two of us—sliced tomatoes, bread, a hard-boiled egg apiece—and I set out two glasses in case she drank wine.

I was trying out all the chairs in her living room, bouncing a little in each, when she came back. She laughed when she saw me and seemed pleased by my efforts toward lunch. She added a half a chocolate cake to my collection, and we sat down across from one another. I guess I must have gobbled my food rather too fast, but she only put the cake and a clean plate before me and said to help myself.

Why didn't she ask any questions? Once my stomach was filled my mind took up its wondering. Maybe she was waiting for me to tell her. I tried, but there was not much I could say without uncovering my wickedness, so I sat silent.

"You will make a very good artist," she said, realizing she would have to do most of the talking.

This didn't help. I remembered how I had once hoped that Monsieur Michel would teach me to draw, show me how he mixed his paints on his beautiful palette, and maybe someday let me try with a real brush. A tide of shame engulfed me. How could I have consented to steal what meant the most to him, no matter for what reason, even that Drollant would be rescued? And now Eel had Mago in his claws forever, and Monsieur Michel would never forgive me even when I told him the truth.

The teacher seemed to vanish as I relived the whole disaster.

"But you look sick, child," I heard her say from a distance. "You must rest here. When I finish my day, we'll decide what is best for you." She gathered up the dishes and set them in the sink. "Goodbye for a few hours. I will look forward to your being here when I get back."

She left without my being fully aware of her going.

What would Mago say now, if he were here to advise me? Even his voice seemed to have deserted my memory. My own voice from the inside told me I had to leave.

Sadness dragged at my legs as I went, but before I closed the door on this woman's kindness, I picked one of her peonies and laid it on the kitchen table. If only I could have written her a note! But maybe she would understand that the flower was my thank you. I left a kiss in the center of the peony.

Ten

THE COMFORT OF THE TEACHER and her house enclosed me all the rest of the day. The way things were, twisted like the rope that had almost made me a slave, I would never be free to accept the teacher's wish to help me, not hers or anyone else's. But I would keep those few hours like a treasure in a box and open the lid to look again when the need to remember arrived.

It was not until the thickening of darkness that the colors of those chalks and the certainty of her liking of me began to fade. I passed by many houses that were strung infrequently along the sides of the road, still somehow tainted by my terror of the witch-woman. But I paused in front of one to listen to the dogs barking inside the cottage. They sounded happy. I peeked between the slits of a shutter, and what I saw banished my memory of fear.

Two old people, a man and a woman, sat at the foot and the head of a round table. And occupying three chairs to their left and right were three dogs, big ones, black and brown and a shaggy little gray one. Before all five was a plate piled with food. The man and the woman had their heads bent, but the dogs had their noses in their dinners, not yet eating but eager.

At a word from the woman they shoveled into the piles.

I waited until all the plates were clean and then knocked on the door.

The two people opened it to me, the dogs properly and politely behind.

"Who are you?" the woman asked.

"I'm traveling south," I answered.

"And you wish a bed for the night?" asked the man.

"I'll work for it."

"Work? A little mite like you?"

"Wait," said the woman. "She could shepherd the dogs tomorrow in the forest. Then you could rest the whole day."

"I would like that," admitted the man.

Not half an hour later I was stretched out within the softness of those quilts, my stomach refilled and drowsiness heavy on my eyelids. The two people said goodnight, the dogs sniffed at me in a friendly way, and I heard nothing more until I felt a nudge under my right ear and opened my eyes to sunlight.

Two paws rested on my arm. I gazed straight into the eyes of the gray dog, the smallest of the three. I pushed back the covers, got up, folded the blankets, and entered the kitchen where the woman was stirring a pot of porridge. Again the dogs sat with us, lapping up the brown cereal almost as hungrily as me.

When we had all finished, the man handed me a sandwich and the three dogs on their leashes. "I have instructed them to obey you," he said.

"You are to take them into the forest and release them. They like to hunt. When it is time to return, simply blow this whistle, snap their leashes on again, and come back. We will expect you at sunset."

The distance to the forest was only about a kilometer, but to me, entering that first stand of trees so tall even a giant couldn't have looked over the tops of them, it was so different I might have walked into another world. Oh, I had been in parks where the grass is trimmed down flat, the flowers planted in designs, the water held in a fountain of stone, and all the trees in planned rows. But nothing like this wonder of wildness.

I stayed very still so that even the rustle of the little bushes that brushed against my legs wouldn't interrupt the waves of sound from the leaves. I felt dwarfed.

Then the three dogs, tugging at their leashes, pulled me forward, and I followed them all the way into the woods. Now I was surrounded, knee deep in greenness. I released the animals, and in three seconds they were gone.

For an hour I wandered slowly nowhere, touching the ridges of tree bark, sometimes stirring the undergrowth with the toe of my shoe to glimpse the underneath. Once I lifted myself onto a low branch of a tree that smelled like the parlor of the orphanage at Christmas. I chewed on one of its spikes and felt I had become a cousin to it as I swallowed the turpentine-tasting needle. I ate my bread and cheese beside a stream whose voice had led me to its banks, and afterward I took off my shoes and socks and dabbled my feet in its coolness. Once a fish slithered over my toes and made me laugh.

I guess maybe all this newness used up my energy because I was not aware of going to sleep until I awoke.

The far-up slivers of sunlight had vanished, and a

streak of red told me the sunset had begun. Hurriedly I blew three blasts on the whistle and waited.

Both the black and the brown dogs tore through the trees at full speed. I clipped on their leashes and blew again. Then a third and a fourth time. Only the muted murmur of the leaves answered the call.

After ten more tries, I made a decision. With the two dogs panting at my heels I led them back to the farmhouse. I only paused to hand them over to the man, and without explanation other than "I'll be back with the gray one," I turned and raced into the forest.

Now it was dark. Drifts of moonlight grayed the tree trunks. For a few moments I imagined I was drowned in silence, but as I listened sounds as small as a light fall of gravel on pavement emerged. Faint stirrings came from the undergrowth, and a ruffling among the leaves, accented by the occasional notes of birds, pushed back any chance of fear. This strange place was alive, as living as I, and I became enfolded. I lifted my arms and was enchanted into a tree. I cast a branched shadow.

An owl hooted above me, and the spell dissolved. I must find the dog! I no longer had the whistle, a stupidity I hated myself for. So I began to call. Not knowing the animal's name, the best I could do was cry, "Here I am! Here I am!"

The scufflings and bird songs ceased. I had cracked the pattern of the night forest. Now, instead of me being the listener, they were. I hoped with my whole self that the little dog could hear me and come; but no bark met my calling, no eager running to join me.

I began to tramp in any and all directions like a lost person, always calling. Then, just when I was ready to flop down on the ground and give up, I heard a kind of whimpering that came from a mass of high vines. I parted the outer strands, pricking my hands on their thorns, and saw the little gray dog hopelessly tangled, crouched in the center. I withdrew and came back with a stick. I prodded the vines apart, holding them down with my feet, and reached in. He licked my hand but refused to come out, so I grabbed him by the scruff of his neck and pulled. Wiggling and whining, he let me lift him through the thicket.

I held him close to me for a long time and stroked him until he quieted. Then I put him down, and we walked together out of the witnessing forest.

The man and the woman opened the door before I had time to knock. They must have been watching from the windows.

The woman slapped the dog hard with the flat of her hand, and when I tried to explain, she slapped me. I turned my back on both of them so that they couldn't see the tears that filled my eyes, and then I left.

I was glad to be on the road again, although I knew that for the rest of the night a ditch would be my bed. It wasn't long before I chose one. The grass grew high and gave me at least a kind of screen from the chill. I wished myself back in Mago's room and imagined he had just lighted the fire and we were about to share three sausages, but the vision was only strong enough to make me so sad my throat ached. I closed my eyes and swallowed. Mago wouldn't want me to feel this way. He believed in laughter, no matter what. I put myself to remembering one day when he had come in from performing, his feet burning with the terrible cold, his eyes stung into streaming, and he had stretched his mouth down with his fingers like a tragic clown and then hopped twice around the room in a kind of mockery of grief. I had laughed so long he got caught up in it too, and we had rolled on our stomachs until weakness stopped us.

I had an odd feeling, lying huddled in that damp ditch, that Mago knew that very minute what I was thinking and that he was proud of me. Right in the middle of a smile, something soft plopped onto my chest. It was the little gray dog! He licked my face all over, even my ears, and now my laughter was real.

Eleven

I WAS STIFF when the first light got me up, except where the gray dog had warmed my side. I hobbled while he trotted, but gradually his jaunty pace quickened mine. What would I call him? I had never heard his name. This reminded me of Mago's and my first meeting when he christened me Cigarette. I caught up with the little animal and began to talk to him.

"I wish you could tell me why you followed me," I said.

His head cocked as he looked up and listened. His eyes seemed to smile, as though he were telling me why and that it was all right if I chose a name.

"How about Trotte?" I asked him.

His tail wagged, so I took that for his consent.

We walked a lot that morning, just to the edge of the first town, and soon I was not aware that he couldn't speak my language. We understood each other. I wonder now, thinking back at all that happened later, if maybe in some mysterious way Mago sent him to me. *Le bon Dieu* knew, I would need him.

I realized, too, as we walked the pavements, passing shops and houses and garages and two parks, that now I was responsible not only for myself but for Trotte. We both had to sleep and eat and keep going, and to do this we needed money. I would take no more chances of stopping in random places like the witch-woman's.

At that moment Trotte came to a halt, lowered his head into a gutter, and came up with a battered lily between his teeth. He waited for me to take it. I did, and sniffed the dying fragrance just to please him.

Low laughter sounded above us. There stood a tall woman dressed in black in the doorway of a shop filled with flowers. For an instant the multitude of colors and shapes blinded me to the person. That window was like a cloud of rose and yellow, white and red, blue and lavender.

Then she spoke, and now her voice held the same tones as Mago's when he said I was looking particularly wispy. "I was just wanting a croissant with my coffee," she was saying. "Will you buy it for me and one for yourself? The baker is directly down the street." She pointed to a shop half a block away and handed me three coins before I could answer.

"I'll have a bone for your dog," she added.

As I bent down to pat Trotte for the gift of the flower she turned back into her shop, and I overheard her murmur, "*La pauvre petite,* I hope she uses the money wisely."

I knew then that she didn't expect me to come back. She thought I would run off with the money. I might have. I'm not like Mago's lady, always present and helpful, and after all I was a thief. I could feel my cheeks redden as I entered the bakery and paid for the rolls, feeling as though the word *thief* had been tattooed on my forehead.

The flower woman was still there, as though her brown

hair and green eyes and skin as bleached as moonlight had been painted against the darker background of her hallway. My fingers itched to have those chalks.

"But what is it, child?" she asked as I stood staring up at her. "You're not afraid of me, surely? Come in. The coffee is hot."

I followed her into a corridor of pale wood paneling that led into what must be a dining room because it was centered by a round table. Only two chairs were drawn up to it. I guessed she lived alone.

"Yes," she said, reading my thought, "I am a widow. One of these chairs is yours."

I don't know why that made me so suddenly happy. I imagined what it must be like for someone to have always had a chair, a place reserved just for her. I fell farther into this fantasy and imagined a room, maybe in the attic, with curtains at the sides of one window. And under that would be a ledge I would sit on and watch the sky change.

She led me to the chair and then brought in the pot of coffee and two cups. The croissants were already on two plates, a lump of butter beside each of them.

She gave Trotte a bone and a saucer of milk in the kitchen and then sat down at the table with me.

I smiled and figured Trotte was smiling too. Why not? For as long as this welcome lasted, I knew then it would be something to remember. There was a kind of silent conversation going on between the lady and me as we ate and drank, and when she spoke it was not an interruption.

"You may be wondering why I invited you into my home. I'll tell you why. You look like I did when I was your age. Even your ears. My name is Celeste Bruneau. And yours?"

"I have a funny name," I began. "A boy gave it to me last year."

She didn't show surprise, just interest.

"He's my real friend." The words came out without my having planned to say them, and it was such a relief to talk about Mago I couldn't stop. "His name is Mago and he adopted me from an orphanage and took me to live in his house and we've been together ever since. He's a lot older than me—maybe fourteen. I don't believe he knows exactly." I paused.

"I understand," she said very quietly. "He's your family."

The rightness of this struck me hard. I wanted to do something so different I shocked myself. I wanted to get up and hug this strange person. Maybe she caught this impulse, though I didn't so much as move a toe because she reached across the table and patted my hand.

"I'm glad you have one," she said.

Her touch made me shy. "My name is Cigarette," I offered in a blurred voice. "You see, Mago said I wasn't very tough and I'd have to learn to earn money acting and singing with him in the streets, and I guess he thought a name like that would give me confidence."

"It's a very pretty name, even if unusual." She got up. "But I must go to the shops and buy you a pair of jeans and a jacket that will cover your bones better than that raveled sweater. Wash yourself and then go into the shop and watch it for me until I get back. If customers come, tell them to wait for me or inquire what they want. Your intelligence will guide you."

No one had ever called me intelligent before. But did she mean I was to stay on? She didn't explain anything, but after she had shown me the downstairs bathroom that had four towels in it and a tub as long as a bed and gone out, I returned to the dining room and sat in my chair again to think.

Maybe it was seeing all those flowers or the way the chair curved into my back or just because somebody liked me, but I went into a kind of trance, like the carnival people who stick pins into themselves and don't feel them. I saw myself before a blank white wall with my left thumb through the hole in a palette, the right holding a brush. And there I was filling the wall with grass so green it made me thirsty and bushes all the sizes I had walked through in the forest with some of Madame Bruneau's flowers rising up between. I was just about to start on the tree leaves when a voice said, "But you haven't bathed!"

I heard myself answer, "No, I haven't finished the trees."

Her laughter brought me back.

"I guessed you were full of imaginings." She was still laughing, but it was a kind sound. "Now, come along."

I followed her into the bathroom.

"I'll just put your new clothes on this stool," she added as she left, closing the door.

First I just looked at the little pile: undershirt and pants, jeans with pockets, a shirt as red as a poppy, a jacket that matched the jeans, and on top of it all a pair of red socks. I reversed their order just for the pleasure of handling each one.

Then, after turning on the faucets full force so that the water gushed like a fountain into the bathtub, I shed my own soiled layers, and even before the water was as high as my feet, I rolled into it. I let it get up to the middle and then I sort of wallowed, the way I'd seen pigs do in mud. I splashed a little too, but not so loud that she would hear me being childish. The soap was fun too. All frothy with bubbles that made rainbows. But best of all was putting on my new clothes. After I had buttoned the last button of the jacket, I stood in front of the mirror and gazed into it for a long time.

What was inside might not be much, but the outside was that of a somebody. For the first time in my life I knew I could go anywhere, like the lobby of the Paris opera house, and not be thrown out. Maybe even Mago, seeing me stroll down the street, would have to be told who I was. That made me giggle.

I bundled my old things under my arm and went down the hall and into the shop.

Madame Bruneau fitted right into my feelings. She half bowed and said, "Good morning, mademoiselle. May I show you some carnations today?"

I suddenly felt timid. I guess I wasn't used to looking like somebody.

She quickly dropped the pretending and became practical. "For the rest of the day," she said, "I want you to get to know my house, and you can sit in the shop and watch how my business is conducted. I'll be very busy, so I'll let you make your own lunch and then we'll talk again at supper time."

Was she leaving the gate open so that, if I wanted to take off, to go on my way without paying after she had bought me all these new things, I could? Was she testing me? Why was she treating me like a first cousin she had known ever since I was born?

I nodded and turned away from her so that she couldn't see the thoughts on my face.

"I have several errands in town. Your room will be on the third floor. Do go up now and see if you like it."

This certainly sounded as though she meant that I could stay, at least for a little while. Or was she giving me an escape hatch, an easy means of no thanks due and be gone? I had all day to get out.

Somehow the stiffness of my jeans and jacket and the wonderful store smell of them—which told me every time I moved that these were my clothes from the very first, not handed down from other bodies—seemed to melt away, to soften as my worry increased. I did as she suggested and mounted the two flights of stairs, Trotte following. I didn't even glance into the two rooms on the second floor.

But when I arrived, I was stopped on the doorsill. This was mine, mine from the rose spread on a bed roofed by the slant of the eaves to the square table so waxed the top looked like a layer of glass, and finally to the window with a ledge wide enough for sitting on so that I could watch the changes of the sky. My wish had become miraculously real.

Then the room blurred. Maybe this was too perfect. Maybe I was making up what I wanted, reading feelings to suit myself. Maybe being all dressed up like this was changing me, unraveling all that I had learned from Mago, that life was hard and bruises permanent.

I did sit on that ledge, and I did face the morning sky, now towered with clouds; but I couldn't accept any of it. And my skin began to prickle from being so clean.

Of course Madame Bruneau didn't mean for me and

Trotte to live here. For a night or two and then down the road, better off thanks to her gifts, but not belonging. I mocked myself for my stupidity and went downstairs to watch her shop. We'd go after dark. She'd have no way of tracing us with a night's head start.

I didn't indulge in any more mind painting as I sat in the middle of those shelves of flowers. I shielded myself from their colors and scents as best I could, though it wasn't exactly easy, especially from the violets; but I must have done a half-good job of it because when Madame Bruneau came back her face suddenly saddened, and I knew it was something about me that caused it. Maybe she guessed my doubts.

The rest of the day was so busy for her that she didn't even join me in a sandwich at noon. I ate alone at the big table, Trotte at my feet, instead of in the kitchen. I was careful not to drop any crumbs, pretending that this had happened every day since I was able to sit up by myself. Maybe a sister and a brother had sat with me, and we'd squabble a bit while our mother was cooking the omelette, and then we'd revert to playing ladies and gentlemen with an occasional sly kick under the tablecloth. I hadn't entered this game since I lived at the orphanage. With Mago I never needed it. Why was I doing it now? Because of this house, that room in the attic, the woman who had cared enough to buy me new clothes?

Then I recognized what was wrong. I was falling into weakness, into that dream world where nothing ever came true and you only walked out of it drearier than before. It was like imagining a feast when you were too hungry. Your mouth soured on nothing to swallow.

That afternoon Madame Bruneau asked me to sweep

out the arranging room where the sink was and the pails of extra flowers that weren't in the shop, but that wasn't much. I spent the time until she drew down the shutters and locked the door sitting on a stool where I couldn't be seen from the front. No use making myself a nuisance. I guessed that there was no place for me and Trotte.

Supper was potato soup, cold meat, beans, salad, and fruit. At first Madame Bruneau talked about the people who had come in during the day, but when I found it difficult to respond, she became silent.

It wasn't until she was peeling herself an orange and me an apple that she looked at me gravely and said, "Are you unhappy here?"

That was such a big question I nearly choked on my bite of apple. Hastily I shook my head. I didn't want to hurt her.

"You don't wish to stay?" was her next question.

"I can't," was all I could blurt out.

"Why?"

There was a pause as wide as a field. Then I plunged into it. "You bought me these clothes, and I can't pay for them. I need money." This was only half the truth. I needed a stake to get me to Chataignier.

She smiled. "But you will earn them. For a long time, the work has been more than I can handle. I will welcome your assistance."

I was stunned. All my certainty of believing she had offered Trotte and me a refuge only for a few days vanished. She did want us. The room would be mine. The chair I sat in would be my place, and soon my clothing would cease to be a gift. And what was left over from my earnings I would save for the journey. For now I didn't want to think about that journey. At least for a little while, Trotte and I had a home.

She was waiting for my answer. All I could manage was a vehement nod, and that was immediately understood.

"Can you read maps?" she asked later as we went up the stairs.

I remembered my success with the map in the Paris window and said, "Yes."

"Then you will be more than useful. You will make all the deliveries in the town. You'll soon become acquainted with the streets. Does that please you?"

I started up my flight of stairs with Trotte at my heels. "I don't know yet, but I will do it," I said.

I wondered why she laughed as she said goodnight and went into her bedroom.

That evening, before I got into my bed, I gave the stars only one quick glance. They would be there the next night and the next, and so would I.

Twelve

THE TWO WEEKS THAT FOLLOWED were like getting into a chair just a little too big for me and pushing myself an inch or so in all directions until the chair became a nest.

Those inches weren't always easy. The morning Madame Bruneau handed me that city map and pointed to my first delivery she found out I couldn't read. Now she would know me to be a liar. The fact that I was something worse—a thief—didn't lessen my apprehension. Would she tell me to leave? Had my foolishness cost me what I had gained, the opportunity to earn enough money to go on? What else I would lose I barred thinking about. I couldn't look her in the eyes.

She spared me. "But that's nothing to be ashamed of," she said.

I wasn't ashamed, but this was not the moment to clear that up. Books had never been close to me because I'd never been able to get inside one. They were for other people.

Again she heard my thought. "You'd like reading. I'll teach you. But, for now, just count the blocks and watch the curves as they are drawn. See? Here is the first house for today. They ordered asters." She traced my route with her finger, then handed me a long white box tied around with a silver ribbon. "Take your time and get to know the town."

I loved those days of going with my boxes of flowers through the streets that started straight and then got mixed up with two or three others, forming triangles in the middle of crossings, usually with a tree or two stuck on them. And sometimes they formed half-circles before they led back into themselves.

Trotte always went with me. We lost our direction over and over, but this too was part of the adventure. And when I returned in time for lunch—we ate quickly in the back room—I dusted and swept the rooms we lived in. The afternoons were more peaceful. While Madame Bruneau did her errands I was the shopkeeper, taking orders on the telephone (I had to memorize them since I couldn't write yet) and answering what questions I could about prices and assortments of flowers.

But the best slice of the day was when the "closed" sign was put out and she and I went into the kitchen and made our supper. We didn't always eat in the dining room. Sometimes the kitchen seemed cozier, especially since that was where Trotte ate too. He never begged for scraps, but I did give him tiny bits just so he'd feel included.

Then it was the reading hour. I'd open to the page where we'd left off the night before, and with the aid of my finger underlining the words as they came, I'd find myself reading. Oh, very simple things about going up in swings (I never had), and how many dolls Fleurette owned and served tea to, and what her mother told her about being a good girl. All rather funny. But I didn't laugh because what I wanted most of all was to leave Fleurette behind and open the other books on Madame Bruneau's shelves, the ones in red and brown leather with gold edges.

Her customers soon got used to me, and once in a while I'd be asked in and given a cup of cocoa or a small roll filled with hidden chocolate. Several asked if she and I were related, expecting me to be a cousin or even a niece, and since I couldn't say she had just picked me off the street, I'd tell them that I was visiting. Trotte was a favorite with everybody, and strangers would stop to pat him and ask his name. He liked that a lot and wagged his tail twice as fast as usual.

Dear Trotte! I remember how he would nudge me awake every morning with his nose and then stand back to see if my eyes would open. Sometimes I'd tease him and pretend I hadn't felt his summons, and he'd try again. By the third time I was laughing and so, I think, was he.

Then the two of us would sit on the window ledge and look out. I never closed the shutters so that those ever-shifting sky colors were always there in that square of glass, even when I was absent. I thought of them as a series of paintings, thousands upon thousands of them, that no artist would ever record. Not even Monsieur Michel would have been able to hold one still long enough to catch.

But through all this unfamiliar happiness—and that is what it was—strode the ghost of my guilt, staining the serenity of Madame Bruneau's warmth, a shadow imprinted on the very walls of my attic, following me along the sides of the houses, never quite out of sight.

Mago was still under the thumb of Eel, and maybe

Drollant wasn't getting well in that clinic, and perhaps Michel had returned to Paris and knew that his green lady had been stolen and had set the police to look for me.

The morning I woke from a nightmare where all these worries had clustered into a bowl of worms that I had to eat or die, I knew I had to leave. Even Trotte seemed to sense a difference and didn't play his game but licked my face as I sat up in bed.

And as I joined Madame Bruneau for breakfast she, too, contained her usual smiling. And when she spoke, her voice was low. "In all the time we have shared you have told me very little about yourself except that you have a friend named Mago and that he has a friend whom he takes care of."

She raised her hand as I started to speak. "No. Even if you had told me nothing, it would have been enough. But today I sense that you are going."

I could only nod my head. I wanted to tell her everything—about the stolen painting, the money and why we had to have it, Mago's enslavement, the whole disaster. I wanted to so fiercely that I had to clamp my teeth together to keep the words back. But I couldn't. She would hate me forever.

"I am sorry. I've been lonely a long, long time, and your being here banished that. But I shall be less lonely now." She got up, going into the small room that adjoined the kitchen, and came back with a box. It wasn't flower size, but more like a present.

I lifted the lid very slowly, not wanting to see what was in it because that would be the end, a kind of seal on my going. Then I saw the purple and blue stripes of the knitting, and when I drew it out, it was a thick sweater with a roll collar that I could pull up over my ears.

"I've been making it at night after you went to bed. The days begin to be cold and will be colder. Your jacket won't be warm enough. Do you like it?"

She didn't have to ask. I already had it on and had buried my nose in the collar. The color of the purple was so intense it seemed to smell of violets, and the blue was the sky from my window.

Trotte, who had been sitting politely by my chair, now put his paws on my leg and sniffed too, his tail in motion.

We all laughed.

"I will miss Trotte too," she said, and her sadness returned. "But wait, child. I've yet to give you your salary. You've become so much a part of my household, I'm afraid I forgot."

I wished I could simply refuse the money, tell her at least a whisper of the joy I had found there, the joy I didn't deserve. But I needed the money to finish my plan, so I said nothing.

She left the room and came back with a tiny cloth purse patterned by worn-off marguerites. She tucked it into the pocket of my jacket. "This should take you a fair way," she said. She looked down at me and then, almost abruptly, as though she were breaking through some kind of restraint, she leaned above me and kissed me on both cheeks.

For the first time in my life, I felt completely protected. Just for that moment. But I was so entirely safe it was as if I were clothed in sunlight.

"I must go out for a while," she said, now at the door. "I

93

may never see you again, but I will never forget you."
With that she was gone.

There I sat, stupid with such a longing to stay that I had
to count myself up those two flights of stairs in order to
make my legs obey. Trotte was just as slow behind me.

Once in the room, my room, I didn't have to collect my
belongings, not having any. I just put on my new sweater
under my jacket, squeezed the little purse to be certain it
was where she had put it, and then I saw the note.

I had learned to write my name, and there it was on an
envelope in Madame Bruneau's handwriting that was as
beautiful as a drawing. I drew out the single sheet of
paper. More words. The lines wavered. I blinked, but that
didn't help. I wiped my eyes dry and carefully slipped the
note back into the envelope and into my other pocket.
Later, much later, I would try to read it.

Then I sat down at the table and took a sheet from the
notebook she had given me to practice writing. I gripped
my pencil tight between my fingers. Twice I pressed down
so hard that the pencil point pierced the paper. The
words I could print were so few I wanted to beat my fists
on the wood. I did what I could and then read back that
miserable, single line: *Dear Madame, I say goodbye, but this
day and tomorrow I say good morning.*

My name at the bottom came out all crooked, so I wrote
it again.

I left the paper where she would see it right away and
ran with Trotte beside me as fast as I could out of her
house.

Thirteen

THE AFTERNOON WAS HALF OVER before I decided
to rest by the road. At noon I had bought a bowl of stew
for Trotte and me at a carnival, but we hadn't lingered. I
was worried that I might have stayed too long with
Madame Bruneau. I did ask several workers how far it was
to Chataignier, but none of them had ever heard of it. I
had an offer for Trotte from the man at the shooting
gallery whose face was tight with meanness, and I
wondered what he wanted with a dog. Neither Trotte nor
I waited to find out. I knew then that I wouldn't trade him
for a shower of gold pieces. We belonged together.

The stone I was sitting on had been warmed by the sun,
and I closed my eyes to better hear the flutter of the leaves
in the poplar trees. I rested one hand on Trotte, who was
stretched out flat in the grass. The peace was so complete
that when it broke with a screech, I almost fell from the
rock.

A low, sleek car had swerved from the highway just
beyond me, and the rubber from its tires marked where it
had gone off. The driver was so still I quickly went over to
him. His hands were clenched on the steering wheel, his
back rigid, but as I put my hand on his shoulder he turned

as sudden as a snake and flashed such a smile I knew he had stopped for a purpose and that I was it.

"You lost?" he said. If his question was meant to be kind, his voice didn't match it.

"No."

"Going somewhere?"

"Yes."

I was still listening to how he was and liking him less and less. Then I asked, not knowing just why, "Is this car yours?"

A curious, hard laugh scraped from his throat. "Not so innocent as you look, are you? Well, it's mine for now. That satisfy you?"

It did. I was experienced enough, no matter what Eel had said about me so long ago, to recognize him for a thief. But, after all, his life was not my affair.

"Going south?" he asked.

I nodded.

"Want a ride partway?"

"Why did you stop for me?" I was curious to see what he would invent. I was sure he would lie.

He became suddenly handsome with charm, the kind you see on billboards, the faces pushing out at you, too big, too unreal. "Tell you what, mademoiselle. You look like a nice child, and it's dull with only me for company."

I kept my expression blank.

He tried again. "The truth is you remind me of my little sister. She's got special looks, like you. Made me lonely for her seeing you there with your dog, so content with each other. How about it? Be a sport. Why not pretend for an hour or so that you really are my sister. That'll save you walking and me a fit of depression."

He was partly right. Even a few kilometers in his fast car would cut some of the distance between me and Monsieur Michel, and I did need to hurry. And if I didn't accept, I would never know why he was insisting. I sensed that he meant no harm to me. Not personally, that is. Instead I would fit into some plan of his. But how?

I called Trotte, and we both climbed in beside him.

With a push of speed we careened onto the highway. He began to whistle through his teeth as he accelerated so fast the poplars flashed by too rapidly to see. Trotte burried his nose in my jacket and sort of trembled against me. I lifted him in my arms and held him very close. Maybe he was wiser than me, and I never should have said yes to this stranger.

I kept staring at his profile, so absorbed in trying to puzzle out why he seemed so familiar that I must not have listened as he talked.

Finally he turned his head and his eyes were ugly. "Tight-lipped, aren't you?"

Now I knew. He was the same kind of person as Eel. Twist your arm and not care if it broke.

I tried to smile. I wanted to get out of that car, to be rid of this dangerous twin to Eel.

We headed into a town, and I hoped that maybe when he slowed down or stopped for a traffic light I would be able to hop down. I was still holding Trotte. But the man did a very odd thing. Instead of driving directly through, he swerved into the outskirts and edged his way past empty lots and isolated houses.

When we were once again on the highway, I asked, "Why did you do that?"

His hands tensed on the wheel. "Reminds me of my

deprived childhood." His voice was harsh with bitterness.

I hadn't any idea what "deprived" meant, and I didn't want to know, but he went into such an explosion of words that I couldn't evade listening.

"I damned every day I was alive in that house. She locked me in a closet if I so much as moved, from the time I was two and could stand up. Later she beat me or stuffed me with sweets and pastries, like they were her apology to herself for being so cruel. She dressed me like a lord. Even bought me a pony. But never sent me to school. I had a tutor just as strict as she was. Then one day—"

The words halted as though his windpipe were cut through. Just in front of us was a roadblock, five policemen beside it.

The man slowed to a stop, then pinched my wrist and hissed at me. "You're my kid sister, remember?"

The pain through my wrist bones was reminder enough.

The officers asked to see his license, then questioned where he had come from and where he was going. He told a very slick tale of how he was taking me to our grandmother in Nice because I had been sick; that he worked for a bank in Paris.

I could tell that my being there swung their opinion in his favor. After many politenesses on both sides, we took off again.

When he had put a few miles between himself and the roadblock, he slowed down in front of a giant park filled with oaks and elms where the distance showed a house larger than a Paris hotel. Without a word, he leaned across me and Trotte and flung the door open.

We didn't waste a second. We had our feet on the grass,

the door slammed, before his feet touched the gas pedal.

"Happy castle!" he called back as he sped away.

I held Trotte against my face for a long moment until my heartbeats slowed, and his too.

Then he barked twice and wriggled free in time to run from a very large white hound that was coming at him like a bullet. Before I could even begin to chase after them, Trotte had turned the tables on his enemy. The hound stood, a cowering lump, while my suddenly little gray demon of a dog raced around him in snarling, snapping circles. There was a yelp of pain as Trotte dove in to deliver a nip to the flank, and then the two of them were streaking so swiftly across the expanse of ground I had only a second to witness Trotte leap the terrace wall of the castle and disappear into an open glass door on the heels of a white flash.

I ran down the long driveway, calling his name, but the wide glass doors merely showed their emptiness to me. I came to a halt standing just below the terrace. I called again, a little less loudly. No Trotte. I tiptoed to the threshold and peeked in, alert to retreat.

I gasped. Without thinking, I stepped all the way inside. What a room! The blue ceiling was painted all over with plump, winged babies dodging clouds and roses, and the silk walls were hung with brownish, deeply framed paintings of meadows, trees, and ponds, among which grazed or rested tiny figures of cows and sheep. There were curtains that fell from the ceiling to the floor, of so deep a red I felt that if I touched one my hand might vanish. The chairs and tables, too, were dark and heavy; and I counted twelve lamps, each with a different shade, all with string fringes.

But it was the fireplace that held me still. I put my hand on the back of an armchair that was almost as tall as I was and stared. Where Mago's and my fireplace in Paris still had a fragment of plaster grapes to enjoy, this was garlanded from one end to the other with flowers and leaves and fruit chiseled from the stone, and up each side climbed a swirl of stone ivy. The mantel was marble, and what rested on it drew me, unthinking, within a foot of its beauty. The golden beast was long, like a giant lizard covered all over with scales of blue and green that even in this dim light shone as I imagined sapphires and emeralds, though I'd never seen any. And from his mouth plumed scarlet flames of the same shining.

I was jerked from this enchantment by a tug at my pants. I looked down into the face of a man as ancient as a tree, seated in an armchair.

I could easily have freed myself; his fingers were no more than brittle twigs. But his eyes were so happy, I just waited.

He coughed, then said, "Emeline, you've come back! Play for me."

I couldn't guess his meaning.

"You remember—the song I loved best."

I looked again around this enormous room and then I saw the piano, not a short stump of one I had seen once in a nightclub but a huge, curved piano that reached far back into the shadows. Its line of white keys divided by the blacks sort of beckoned me. I wondered what their sounds were, maybe full of thunder to match the size of the casing.

He gave me a feeble shove toward my temptation to touch it.

"But I can't play," I said.

"Nonsense. Every evening after dinner you played for half an hour."

I went over to this majestic instrument and placed my thumb on the middle key, then my next finger two keys up, and my little finger up two more. I pressed down.

I will never forget what I heard. It was the artist's palette, daubed with all his colors. It was that hour in the forest when all the trees had voices. It was me and Mago and Drollant on a park bench just being together.

I lifted my hand and sounded the notes again, then a third time.

"No! No!" His crackled voice caused me to snatch my fingers away. "I guess you're not in the mood. Never mind. Come sit beside me. Dear Emeline. You're so very young today."

The pressure of this room, the weight of the furniture, the carpets that seemed to entrap my feet in their softness, the high curtains that blanked out the world beyond the windows, the craziness of the old man; all began to muffle my thoughts, to drug me. I must find Trotte.

Cautiously I walked to the hallway, hearing only a small sigh from within the old man's chair. I looked up at a staircase wide enough for a pair of elephants to pass each other without bumping. And there at the top was Trotte, sniffing at the banister.

I hissed at him through my teeth, but he only glanced at me, his tail moving, and went back to his occupation. I looked past him into the upper hall and saw that the walls were lined with paintings right up to the ceiling. They were each of a person in a costume.

I was about to join Trotte for a closer view when a voice

so furious that it hurt my ears shouted, "Come down from there, you nasty animal!" And at almost the same moment I was seized by the back of the neck.

Trotte came running to rescue me, growling and snarling. He, too, was nipped at the neck and lifted waist high by a big, square man in an evening suit. Trotte struggled like a fish to release himself, his legs churning in the air. With a shake that must almost have loosened his teeth, the man threw him toward the front door. Trotte skidded and struck the wall.

I stamped down on the man's instep, and his grip relaxed. I dashed over to Trotte. He seemed all right, if a bit groggy, but I held him safe in my arms. No one was going to hurt my dog, not ever.

The man was in a rage. "Now get out, both of you, or I'll use force you won't like!"

He started toward us when we all heard the quavery tones of the old man in the chair. "They may come in, George."

Such a change came over the man, who I now realized was a servant, that his clothes might have been inhabited by another person. His face was as white as his shirt, and his powerful shoulders slumped.

"Yes, sir." This time, instead of threatening me, he stood back as I entered that dense room. Nobody had ever stepped back for me before except once when Mago and I were pretending he was a knight and I a queen. We'd seen some pictured when we'd gone into a museum to get warm.

The old man spoke again. "You must never speak harshly to Emeline, George. I forbid it. She has never

102

been quite right. You know—delicate—and now she's come to stay."

"And the dog too, sir?"

"Is there a dog? Well, if it amuses her, the animal shall be our guest. Now bring us tea with plenty of sweet cakes. Emeline is fond of sugar."

George strode off. Trotte and I sat on the rug near the old man and close enough to that beautiful fireplace so that I could study the clusters of fruits and flowers and gaze at the dragon. We'd leave immediately after eating. Being Emeline was beginning to spook me a little.

No one said a word until George reappeared with a silver tray as large as a sled, filled with pitchers and plates. These last were piled up with round pink cakes, ringed with candy violets and leaves. George drew up a table and chair for me and then served us both. I'd never tasted tea before, preferring wine if money had to be paid out, and its flavor reminded me somewhat of tobacco. But I drank half a cupful to be polite. The old man was gulping his in loud slurps. The cakes I ate, three of them, and when George had gone and the old man's nose was deep in his cup, I put one in each pocket for later. Trotte got his share, of course, liking them as much as I did.

I could tell that the old man was getting sleepy by the slowing of his movements as he finished a third cup of tea.

"So happy to have you, Emeline," he said, and then, like a tiny child's, his chin dropped; his eyes closed, and he slept.

I looked once again around that dim, rich room, smiled at the piano for letting me know how it sounded, even just that once, and then Trotte and I scurried like mice from that great, hollow house.

The grass beside the highway seemed doubly green, the sunlight recharged with brightness. I found myself singing Mago's song as we walked through another day.

Fourteen

NEITHER TROTTE NOR I were very hungry after the feast of cakes, but we did share a plate of noodles and chicken in a café at seven o'clock that evening. I was being rather stingy with the money Madame Bruneau had given me. Later there might be a more urgent reason to spend it than stuffing our stomachs.

As we came out of the steamy room I saw Trotte's ears prick up. Then I heard it too. Music, coming from behind the wide doors of a church that looked like a toy copy of the big one in Paris.

We went in—Mago's lady was there as usual—and sat down at the back where we could see the silver pipes of the organ and watch the player's feet jump back and forth on some pedals. Then, for a little while, I forgot to look at anything. I was inside those throaty sounds. I was dancing around and through them, slowly turning and turning.

I must have gone to sleep, Trotte too, because when we woke the music was gone and the candles in front of the lady had burned very low. Only one person was with us, a man all in black kneeling in front of the cross on the platform in the center.

I waited until he got up and then approached him.

"Can you tell me how far it is to Chataignier?" I said right out.

"Only ten kilometers," he answered directly, though his eyes showed some surprise. "You just keep on down the highway."

I thanked him and was about to leave when one more question popped out of me. "What's her name?" Mago had never told me, and anyone important enough to be queening it in every church I'd ever been in had to be called something.

The man gave me a sharp look, as if he suspected me of mocking him. Then he shook his head in astonishment. "You truly don't know, my child, do you? Her name is Mary." He said the word tenderly, the way Madame Bruneau had spoken to me when she said goodbye.

I thanked him once more. Now Mago and I could discuss her if we wanted to, and he'd be pleased that I knew her better.

The man made a funny little sign in the air above my head and then Trotte and I walked into the night. Neither of us was tired, and I'd wasted too much time already to stop again. The dread of not finding Monsieur Michel nipped at my heels and strengthened my legs as we followed the band of moonlight that illuminated the road.

Morning had not quite arrived when we came to the first house of the village. There weren't many more houses to follow, maybe fifty.

The one café was open, and I ordered coffee with lots of hot milk and sugar for both of us. Trotte had his in a bowl.

I started to say, "Do you know where—" and suddenly

106

wondered how to ask for the woman in green who had been Michel's wife.

The proprietor wasn't used to listening to children, so my question simply trailed off into the good smell of coffee.

Then it occurred to me to describe Monsieur Michel. "If you please, monsieur," I began, "can you tell me where a tall man with dark hair who paints pictures and was once married to a lady here in your village lives?"

He made me repeat it all. Then he grinned. "I know who you mean—that crazy artist fellow. Gave his name to Madame Courier and then took off."

I didn't correct his story. "Yes, Madame Courier." Of course. I had been stupid not to think of asking for Michel's wife by name.

"She lives three streets down and to the left. There are two linden trees in front of her house. But what business a mite like you might have with her is tomorrow's news."

I thanked him without offering explanations, and Trotte and I hurried away. The shutters were still closed in all the windows of the long white house behind the linden trees, and the sun hadn't yet reached over the blue slate roof. We sat down on the grass with our backs against the wall that enclosed her garden.

The longer I sat there, the faster my heart accelerated. I knew that Monsieur Michel would never forgive me, would be glad to see me in prison and would never come to visit me. No one would, no one but Mago. Now everything rushed at me, thoughts so dark they obliterated the colors around me. The delphiniums browned, the marguerites grayed. Even the grass seemed to turn black.

Mago was already caged by the wickedness of Eel. Maybe Drollant was in an institution, being treated like a sick animal, unwanted and unfed. And all because of me.

I didn't see the shutters swing forward, folded back. I missed the lady in green as she stood gazing out at me. That is, until she rapped on the glass, beckoning me to go to the front door.

For a moment I just stared at her. She was the painting all over again, only this morning she wore a blue dress. I guess it must have been more than a moment because I was still in the same spot when she reappeared, framed by the threshold of the open door.

I shattered inside. I ran to her, shouting, "Where is Monsieur Michel? Tell him I'm here! Hurry!"

She didn't back away from me but pulled me into the house.

"You're distraught, child! What's the matter? Try to calm yourself and tell me."

I had a terrible feeling that the house was empty behind her. This sent me into further wildness. "You know him! He's your husband! Where is he?"

She managed to get me to a chair and sit me in it. "Of course he is my husband. But he's gone. He left for Paris yesterday. He will be living here now, after he closes up his studio."

The room I never really saw and will never remember spun in faster and faster circles, and then I dropped into nothingness.

I returned, not to the perfumed enclosure of the woman's arms, though they held me upright, not to how beautiful she was—even now, so much later, I can only recall how she was in the portrait, as though I had never seen her at all—I returned to such despair I wanted to faint forever.

She was talking, but her words only half entered my brain: " . . . make tea for you . . . stay quiet . . . right back." What did fall like hailstones, heavy and hurting, were the voices of Mago and Drollant battering the sides of my head, and their words were my own: "Failed . . . you ruined everything . . . we're lost, each of us . . . your fault, all of it."

When she placed the tray on a small table in front of me, the scent of the tea sickened me. She added sugar and offered me a little cake in the shape of a boat.

I shook my head. I couldn't speak. I was choked with such misery I covered my eyes with my fists to blind myself to the world.

She must have removed the table because when she gently forced my hands down from my face, she was kneeling before me.

"You need Michel. I understand that. So do I. I'll not question you as to why. I sense you won't tell me. But I will put you on the noon train for Paris if you reassure me you can travel safely by yourself."

I flung my arms around her neck and began to cry. I think I cried for a very long time because my eyes still stung when she put me on that train an hour later. And we hadn't talked hardly at all. I don't believe I ever thanked her, and as I'll never see her again I hope she knows I meant to. She even found a straw basket with a lid to put Trotte in so that he could ride with me in the compartment. And beside him was a packet of sand-wiches.

I hope I waved goodbye, but I probably didn't. The first

time I remember partly emerging from what was true darkness was at the sight of the town where I had been so foolish as to be happy.

We stopped at the station so long—maybe five minutes —that a kind of fantasy almost put a hook in me. What if I got off the train, showed up at Madame Bruneau's door, and started life all over again? What if, as on that day in the cellar of the orphanage when Mago closed the book on what had gone before and started a new page for me, with a new name and a new reason for living, what if I let Madame Bruneau do the same? I would take another name, a real one. But, sightless in the train compartment, so turned into myself that I don't now know who filled the other seats, when my mind took me into that little room under the eaves, I raced out of it. There would be no true welcome in that house, not for a person like me, not after Madame Bruneau discovered the truth. And, sooner or later, I would have to tell her, or the love between us would be permanently smeared.

Trotte was licking my hand, one paw poking at the package of sandwiches. I was grateful to be pulled away from these imaginings. I ate half of mine and gave Trotte the rest; but to comfort myself for the loss of what I would never have, I closed my eyes and pretended that I was a green plant in Madame Bruneau's kitchen window and that sometimes when she was grinding the morning coffee beans, she would look at the leaves and say to herself, "Cigarette would have liked this one. I wonder where she is."

I felt in my pocket for the note she had left me that I had never tried to read. Those words, whatever they were, were like a last breath of her. If I released them, she would

110

vanish forever. Maybe someday when I was old. But for now they were my talisman. Maybe she had dismissed me with a final goodbye. Maybe she had put love in with them. Secret from me, I could believe she had.

The easement of the letter brought me sleep, and it wasn't until the conductor came through announcing our arrival in Paris that I awoke.

Fifteen

AT FIRST TROTTE was made so nervous by the crowding of cars and people that he cringed against my leg as we hurried across the city to Mago's place. But when we stood together in front of the scabby building, Trotte seemed to recognize it and went ahead of me up the stairs.

I don't know what I expected—Mago standing in the firelight, his arms open to hug me home? A little supper all ready with a full bottle of wine?

There had never been a lock on the door, and when I opened it, the dank blackness of the room threw itself over me like a giant rag, and for an instant I thought I would smother in it. I stepped inside. Trotte began to sniff his way along the baseboards.

Suddenly he squealed, and I heard a thump against the far wall.

"What the devil are you doing here?" came a voice like a razor. It was Eel.

"You kicked my dog!" I yelled into the obscurity.

"Did I now?" That detestable figure slid from the shadows and came so close I could smell his rankness. "And aren't we the lady, though—it'll be a brace of poodles next to accompany your promenades in the park."

Trotte was now leaning against me as I stroked his back.

"Where is Mago?"

A jeer was his answer.

I reached out with both fists and pummeled his chest. "Where is he?"

He slapped my face so viciously I almost lost my balance. Then he turned and went to the mantel. There he lit a thick candle, and now I could see his ugliness clearly. "Mago? Well, I'll tell you. When you deserted him, he got into trouble. He's been in prison ever since you left."

I knew from his sly expression that he was lying. I think he imagined I would break into sobs or some such thing because his grin of enjoyment faded as though it had been washed off. I knew that any insistence would simply encourage him to mock me. I had to find out some other way.

"I guess you know that the painter has returned to Paris," I said.

"So? What's that to me? I'm in the clear. Not you. Not Mago. I stayed out of it, but they know what Mago looks like. The gallery owner described him."

"And how do you know all this?"

"I have my sources," he said smugly.

I wished Trotte were a great dragon that could swallow up this nasty morsel of a human.

Squatting on the floor, he continued to talk. "Now that you're here, you might as well be useful—to me, of course. I could use you as a decoy when I go shoplifting in department stores. You look respectable enough in those new clothes to deceive the saleswomen. Or I could sell what you have on and send you begging in rags. Or I might teach your dog tricks with the aid of a whip and set him to dancing to your singing. How does that appeal to you?"

"I'd be caught the first day," I said.

He nodded. "That's right, you might. Well, I'll invent something for you to do that is profitable to me. You can count on it. Now," he got up—"I'm off to have a little fun. See you tomorrow. Sleep tight."

After he had left, I stuck my head through the sacking over the window and breathed in the frosted night air. It wasn't wine, but it did take the bad taste out of my mouth. Just talking to Eel made me queasy. It was too late to search out Mago now, so I curled up on my old pile of sacks, Trotte beside me, and hoped I would dream of him.

The dreams I woke from were of the witch-woman who had intended to enslave me, only this time I wasn't able to free myself. And because she let my clothes rot off my body, I grew fur, coarse orange fur even over my face and up to my eyes.

I reached out to feel my cheeks and screamed. Then I saw that I had touched Trotte. Breathless, I squeezed him so tight he yipped. What would I do without this little animal so recently a part of my life and now so truly mine? What would I do without Mago?

We paused only long enough to each have a roll dipped in coffee and a hard-boiled egg at the café on the corner before hurrying to Drollant's clinic. He would know where Mago was hiding out.

I silently thanked Madame Bruneau all over again for

114

my new clothes because when the receptionist came to the door I could tell she was impressed by my appearance. Maybe she especially liked the purple and blue stripes of my sweater. In any case she asked me to come in.

"And what may I do for you, mademoiselle?" she asked.

"I'd like to talk to a friend of mine who lives here with you," I replied. "His first name is Drollant." I had never heard that he had a second.

"Yes, I know the boy. But to see him you will have to wait. He is having his breakfast with the other children. He eats very sparingly, so it is best not to disturb him."

She offered me a chair in the hall, and since she had made no objections to Trotte, I chose the largest one and we both sat in it.

Very soon afterward I saw Drollant coming down the long corridor. He seemed to have shrunk two sizes and was hardly wider than the crutches that supported him. I paused to see if he recognized me. With Drollant you never knew what alley his mind had chosen to wander into.

He did. His mouth smiled and then his eyes. I ran to embrace him, but not too hard. He looked very breakable.

"Oh, Drollant, I am so happy to see you!"

I think he meant to say something happy to me too, but suddenly it was Trotte who had his entire attention. So immediate was the bond between them that an onlooker might have thought Trotte was his. Trotte offered his right paw, and Drollant's face became all joy. Carefully he leaned down and shook it.

The nurse who had followed Drollant guided him to a couch and helped him down into it. I sat beside him, and

Trotte didn't need to be invited to enclose his other side.

I began with a simple question. "Where is Mago?"

Drollant turned his head away from the dog for an instant. "Mago? He comes sometimes."

"But where does he live?" I kept my voice calm.

Drollant shrugged, concentrating on patting Trotte's back.

"Please listen, Drollant! I must find Mago, and you're the only one who knows."

A flick of intelligence showed in his eyes. "Except Eel." I could see he was straining. "Eel knows." The information seemed to satisfy him that he had answered me, and I realized this was hopeless.

The nurse had gone, and a matron was standing stiffly in front of us. "You are a friend of the patient?" she asked somewhat sternly.

I had to lie or I'd never find Mago. "I'm his sister," I said.

"Oh, then the other boy who generally comes at noon must be your older brother."

I didn't deny it. Mago was as much of a brother as anyone could ever be.

Her eyebrows raised as if in doubt, but all she said was, "You can't wait here. This young man has a strict schedule to follow."

I wondered if she were going to order me into the street, but she didn't. "You may sit in the garden if you wish."

The atmosphere was anything but summer as I tried a stone bench behind a tree. The chill penetrated through my jeans in two minutes, so I followed Trotte as he explored the paths and bushes.

That's how I missed Mago's entrance. I was just making a turn around a hedge shaped like an enormous pot when a blaze of sun held me light-struck, and in the center of this radiant cone was a figure my eyes mistook for a vision.

The vision spoke. "Cigarette! It's you!"

Mago!

I took those few yards in two leaps. I was total joy. He held me long enough for all the past anguish within me to dissolve. When he released me and as we looked into each other's eyes it was as it had always been between us, he for me and me for him, a kind of certainty that whatever the world dealt out nothing, not the very worst, could dent our friendship.

The moment passed as swiftly as the fall of a stone. His expression became tense with worry. "But you shouldn't have returned, Cigarette. You know what the scene is. The gallery owner has been arrested for selling stolen goods—not a new practice with him. The police are searching for me, thanks to Eel, who informed that I brought the painting to the gallery in order to keep in with the law, though he gave a false description so he could use me. And now Michel Courier is back. He will identify you."

"But why do you come here, Mago? Every time you show yourself, you're in danger."

He smiled, one of those older, wise smiles I knew so well. "I know that, but this morning I'm here to get Drollant. If anything should happen to me, I just can't take the risk that he would be collected by strangers and shut up God knows where for the rest of his life."

"How? How will you manage?"

"Madame Laurier, the laundry lady, is signing him out at noon."

"But where will we go?"

"No, Cigarette, not you. Just me and Drollant. I've got to find him a decent home, a place somewhere outside the city where he can work with a farmer for part of his keep. I've still got my share of the money and will give that over before I leave. But come sit with me. We still have a few minutes."

I obeyed as always.

"Now listen to me and listen carefully. And if you don't quite understand what I am saying, what I mean, you will later. Just memorize the words."

This was old times between us when I was first adopted into Mago's life and knew nothing except that I had a home and someone who cared. I had advanced a long way since then but was aware that I still had a lot to learn, so I was content to do whatever he told me.

"You must stay free, for yourself and for me. You must be my chance—the one I never really had from the beginning."

"Chance?" I had to ask that much.

"Yes, Cigarette, your chance will become mine because I am giving mine to you in this moment. A chance to go to school, to find a place to live where meals are a part of every day, where you'll never have to sleep under dirty sacks or beg your way through the streets, where winter will never hurt you or the rot of summer bring you sickness. You will have to earn this chance, but you must from now on start looking for it, and"—he paused and would not meet my look—"you must do it by yourself."

118

I opened my lips to speak my shock, but before a word formed, he said, "For my sake." That sealed my mouth.

He turned from me. "But who is this?" It was Trotte running toward me, his tail waving.

I swallowed hard and tried to match Mago's attempt at lightness. I introduced the two of them, and Mago squatted down and pretended to be another dog. Trotte's delight made us laugh, and I blessed him for it. At least for now he had blocked off the dreaded future.

But the thought of it was not long in returning. To delay the fact I asked, "But Drollant can't walk yet. How will you get away?"

"I have a handcart in the basement of our house. He'll enjoy the ride." Mago stood up after a final pat for Trotte. He placed his hands on my shoulders. "Now, Cigarette."

I tried to keep my mouth from trembling but couldn't, so I spoke for control. "Remember when you first called me Little Cigarette?"

"I remember." His eyes seemed to have deepened. "But you are not 'Little' anymore."

Hearing Mago say this was a restraint to my tears. If only some magic could have transported us back to before, my pride would have sent me dancing. But there was no sense in making room for such a childish wish. I erased it.

"You must go," he said next, his voice strangely high.

"I can't!" I burst out. "I can't leave you!"

He brushed his hand across his eyes. "No matter what, no matter where," he said, "we will never leave each other."

I understood.

Then he did a last thing to make it easier for me. He turned me about-face and helped me take those first few steps apart from him.

I never looked back. I couldn't. And once away I raced half-blind, Trotte beside me, to Monsieur Michel's studio, to finish off the last act.

Sixteen

HE WAS THERE, but when he opened the door I met a stranger. Not the Monsieur Michel who had talked and laughed and bought me pastries. That Michel was gone, and in his place was an unsmiling sternness that loomed over me. He did not ask me in.

"Why did you come back?" he asked in tones so frozen they made me shiver.

"I had to."

"Oh?" His look scorned me. "There is really no need to confess. You took it. Your comrade sold it. What else is there to say except that you are a fool to come here?"

"Please listen," I said, pushing my way past the barrier of him until I stood in the middle of the loft, Trotte with me. "I have to tell you that I am sorry."

"And that will make it right?"

"No, nothing will ever do that. I am a thief. I deserve to be punished. I'm sorry I took what didn't belong to me, something you treasured. But most of all I'm sorry I betrayed what you gave me."

He sat down on his stool, his severity slightly lessened. "What I gave you?"

"Your friendship."

He glanced at his hands as if they were asking something of him.

"And now you can never trust me again."

His sigh voiced sadness. He said nothing.

"I tried to find you to tell you before."

"I was in Chataignier."

"I know. I went there."

At this his head came up, and he was beginning to lose the strangeness. "You? When? How?"

I told him about the journey, taking a long time to finish. I think this happened because I had wanted to tell Mago, and now I never would. It simply spilled out of me. The only part I skimmed over, not mentioning the best of those days, were those two weeks with Madame Bruneau. I couldn't excuse myself for staying that long, for dropping out of the mess I had created. But I knew why. I had wanted that kindness, that attic, that welcome so desperately that I had to have it. They would never come again, and I would need them to remember.

I guess as I talked I sort of forgot Monsieur Michel, for by the time I came to the end I saw that he had changed back into himself. He was even smiling.

"I am sure you mystified Madame Courier," he said, "arriving like an apparition and then vanishing in a puff of train smoke." He picked up a stub of charcoal and began to draw on his sketch pad. I wondered what my face told him.

"You are an honest creature," he said. "And I have something to be sorry for, too." He paused, as he so often had, not finishing his thought out loud, as though what he was drawing was saying it for him.

"You? You mean because you told the police about me?"

"Yes. I had to. No one else knew where the key was, and there was no evidence of a break-in. They suspected the landlady and were prepared to arrest her. Then they asked me to identify you and I did—with this." He held up the stick of charcoal.

"Then they know what I look like."

"Only too well. I wish now I hadn't, but I was very angry."

I realized as I gazed at the tenderness that was part of his usual expression that it hadn't been all anger. I had hurt him. How had I come to be such a monster?

It was my turn to sigh. "I must go now and turn myself in," I said.

"No, wait. You are a child. You must have a better chance than living your next years in a house of correction. You can go to Chataignier with me. My wife and I are going to live together again."

"I can't. I have to save Mago from prison."

"And sacrifice yourself?"

I didn't understand this and didn't try. I knew what I had to do. Mago came first.

"Besides," he continued, "there is no saving him. He made the sale. A street boy who knew him as well as the gallery owner testified against him."

Eel, that evil, conniving Eel.

I shook my head. "You have to go with me to the police and tell them that I am the real thief, that I forced Mago to present the painting."

"No. That won't do. He'll have to face the consequences of what he did."

I knew Monsieur Michel couldn't see things as they were. He didn't know the facts, why we had to get the

123

money to rescue Drollant, and there was no point in informing him of the truth behind the crime, my crime. I alone had done it. I would have to go to police headquarters by myself, but first I must tell Mago how things stood. And for an instant my heart felt a small rise of joy. I would see him again even if only for the time it took to give him my message.

Trotte and I dashed out of the studio before Monsieur Michel could stop us.

Seventeen

WHAT HAPPENED NEXT I have to tell quickly without any feelings. Even now, so long later, I shove it away in the forbidden corners of my mind if I can. But when it comes back, I play it like the running of a film at doubled speed; and even as it flicks by, my whole self shudders all over again.

I found Mago and Drollant. I found Eel. The three of them were at Mago's place, hunched over what remained of their supper.

For something to say—because Mago was acting oddly, as though the presence of Eel had put a spell over him, a bad spell—I asked, "Why so early?"

"Drollant and I are taking off soon," was Mago's terse reply.

"And Mago has to be back before dark," said Eel, sort of sneeringly.

Mago's face was wooden. "Yes," he said, not meeting my eyes. Then came words I couldn't believe. Not from Mago. "So you get going. You're not welcome here. Never really were."

I heard them, those words, but I didn't accept them. This was the person who had pulled me up out of nowhere and given me a life. From no love at all and no place to find it, he had taken me slowly, day by loving day, to where he was. And from then on, it was together, not me there and him here. He had a reason for this false cruelty. It had to be Eel.

My thoughts were answered by Eel's speaking next. "That's not quite how I see it," he said to Mago. "Glad she showed up. Simplifies things."

"Meaning what?" Mago's voice was stronger now.

"Meaning I'm going to turn her in to the police. That'll give me more than a kilometer of credit with them, and for what I have planned I'll need it. Planned for Mago, that is."

Drollant seemed to sense the tension that was now as fast as a circle of barbed wire around all of us. He began to whimper.

Eel cuffed him, twice. It was Trotte, who had followed me and whom I had almost forgotten, who came to Drollant's defense, not Mago. The little animal growled and went for Eel's ankle. But not before Eel lifted his other foot and booted Trotte across the room.

Mago had not stirred. Not until this moment. He got to his feet and stood very tall in front of Eel. "Cigarette is leaving now, for good. If you so much as touch her, you will regret it."

Eel grimaced with anger. "Regret? What's that? I could slice her six ways and crack her bones in seven with one hand and eat a chicken leg with the other and not care. As for you—you'll begin to call me sir if I demand it! You've no rights, not one; so unless you want a kick where it hurts most, you'll stand back and shut up!"

He made a move toward me, just a small one, and Mago was on him. They wrestled wildly, their elbows and knees thumping against the hollow floor, sometimes Eel on top, sometimes Mago. They were such a tangle I couldn't mix in. Even Trotte had to stay on the fringe of the fight. Drollant was howling in a corner.

Then I saw that terrible glint in Eel's right hand. A knife. The glint vanished. Mago's body arched, and he gave a great cry as he flung himself over onto his back and lay still.

Eel scrambled upright. Staring down at the stream of blood that flowed from Mago's chest, he began to shrink, his face cloud-white. He gave one grunt of "Oh my God!" and fled.

I knelt over Mago, and ripping off my sweater, I tried to bind it around his ribs to stop the bleeding. The purple and blue stripes were dyed so suddenly red I knew he was going, going where for the first time I couldn't follow. For an instant his eyes saw me, and what they said gave me all the glory I had ever known, as though the radiance of those stained-glass windows had entered into him and was surrounding me forever. I was held in his light, in his love. And then the final darkness took him.

What I did next remains blurred to me. I do remember supporting Drollant down the stairs on his crutches, getting him into the handcart, checking to see if Trotte was with us, and wheeling him to the laundry woman's shop. I must have made some sense because she promised to look after Drollant.

I was afraid to do more than give the poor befuddled boy one kiss on the top of his head. I was afraid I wouldn't be able to leave him. His expression was sort of muddied, as though he hadn't understood. But just as I was about to turn from him, he reached out and grabbed Trotte's tail.

Trotte wasn't even startled. He licked Drollant's other hand, and then I knew what else I must lose.

Numbly I asked the laundry woman for a piece of rope, and when she brought it, I tied one end loosely around Trotte's neck, the other to Drollant's cart.

I never looked back.

As I climbed the stairs to Monsieur Michel's studio I was a bundle of sticks strung together like a crude marionette. I had to say goodbye to somebody. I was floating on black air. I was knifed, too, but no blood came out of me, just a slow seepage of breath that wouldn't be lasting long.

I don't know what Monsieur Michel said to me. I waited until his mouth stopped moving, and then I left.

The next place I remember was finding myself on the same bridge that Friquette so many months ago had chosen for her ending. I gripped the iron railing and stared down at the sluggish water below. A skim of oil on the surface made moving rainbows, but they meant nothing to me. I only wondered if it was very cold underneath their shining.

My hands loosened, and I moved forward. Then, suddenly, someone was standing beside me, someone who spoke with Monsieur Michel's voice. The urgency in it made me listen. "Promise me," he said, "promise me you will go back to my studio. I will take care of what you left behind you. I will see that the police are informed, that Eel is picked up."

So I must have told him what had happened, though I had been deaf to my own telling.

Once again he said the words. "Promise me."

I nodded. What he offered was something other than the railing to hang on to. I kept my word.

Eighteen

I BELIEVE I spent a whole week with Monsieur Michel, mostly sleeping when I wasn't hurting so fiercely inside I couldn't eat or talk.

He never interfered. Sometimes, when I could see outside myself, I'd watch him from my cot at his easel, so concentrated I began to be sort of pulled into his connection with what was going onto his canvas.

Then one morning he offered me his palette and his box of oil paints and put a brush in my hand.

"See?" he said, gesturing toward the blank oblong in front of me. "It's all there somewhere."

That was the day when Mago came back to me without any tears.

I never did put colors on that canvas. I could see them, but something told me it was not yet the right time. Monsieur Michel understood. He nodded and said, "Later. I promise you."

Well, now it is later by a year, and he was right. I do paint whenever I have the chance. That word, ever since Mago gave it to me—his chance—has been the light ahead, the light I may someday catch up to.

But this story has to be concluded, the design complete.

The day I allowed Mago to be dead and then to return for all the days of my life, I took the letter I had saved for so long from my jacket pocket.

Before I opened the envelope, I ran my finger over Madame Bruneau's handwriting, sort of like touching her very lightly on the arm, and then I read it. None of the words were a mystery to me.

Dear Cigarette,
    I will be here when you come back.
    With love.

So that's where I am. I go to school. I eat three meals a day. I deliver the flowers Saturday and Sunday. I am loved. I will never again sleep under dirty sacks or beg my way through the streets. Winter will never hurt me or the rot of summer bring me sickness. I have my chance, and I am earning it; but Mago was wrong about one thing. He said I must do it by myself. But it is his chance, too, and we are sharing it together.

BOOK TWO

Sir Arthur Conan Doyle's

THE ADVENTURES OF
SHERLOCK HOLMES

Adapted for young readers by Catherine Edwards Sadler

The Sign of the Four What starts as a case about a missing person, becomes one of poisonous murder, deceit, and deep intrigue leading to a remote island off the coast of India.

The Adventure of the Blue Carbuncle It's up to Holmes to find the crook when the Countess' diamond is stolen.

The Adventure of the Speckled Band Can Holmes save a young woman from a mysterious death, or will he be too late?

Join the uncanny and extraordinary Sherlock Holmes, and his friend and chronicler, Dr. Watson, as they tackle dangerous crimes and untangle the most intricate mysteries.

AVON CAMELOT

**AN AVON CAMELOT ORIGINAL ●78097 ● $1.95
(ISBN: 0-380-78097-6)**

BOOK THREE

Sir Arthur Conan Doyle's
THE ADVENTURES OF
SHERLOCK HOLMES

Adapted for young readers by Catherine Edwards Sadler

The Adventure of the Engineer's Thumb When a young engineer arrives in Dr. Watson's office with his thumb missing, it leads to a mystery in a secret mansion, and a ring of deadly criminals.

The Adventure of the Beryl Coronet Holmes is sure that an accused jewel thief is innocent, but will he be able to prove it?

The Adventure of Silver Blaze Where is Silver Blaze, a favored racehorse which has vanished before a big race?

The Adventure of the Musgrave Ritual A family ritual handed down from generation to generation seemed to be mere mumbo-jumbo—until a butler disappears and a house maid goes mad.

Join the uncanny and extraordinary Sherlock Holmes, and his friend and chronicler, Dr. Watson, as they tackle dangerous crimes and untangle the most intricate mysteries.

AVON CAMELOT

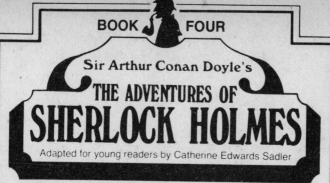

BOOK FOUR

Sir Arthur Conan Doyle's
THE ADVENTURES OF
SHERLOCK HOLMES

Adapted for young readers by Catherine Edwards Sadler

The Adventure of the Reigate Puzzle Holmes comes near death to unravel a devilish case of murder and blackmail.

The Adventure of the Crooked Man The key to this strange mystery lies in the deadly secrets of a wicked man's past.

The Adventure of the Greek Interpreter Sherlock's brilliant older brother joins Holmes on the hunt for a bunch of ruthless villains in a case of kidnapping.

The Adventure of the Naval Treaty Only Holmes can untangle a case that threatens the national security of England, and becomes a matter of life and death.

Join the uncanny and extraordinary Sherlock Holmes, and his friend and chronicler Dr. Watson, as they tackle dangerous crimes and untangle the most intricate mysteries.

AVON CAMELOT

AN AVON CAMELOT ORIGINAL • 78113 • $1.95
(ISBN: 0-380-78113-1)

Dancing means more to her
than anything in the world . . .

Maggie Adams, Dancer
A Novel by
Karen Strickler Dean

Maggie Adams lives in a dancer's world—of strained
muscles and dirty toe shoes, sacrifices and triumphs,
hard work and tough competition. There is little time
in Maggie's life for anything but dance, as her family
and boyfriend come to learn. Her mother spoils her,
her father isn't convinced of her talent, and her boyfriend doesn't understand why he doesn't come first
in her life. But Maggie—spirited, gifted and determined—will let nothing stand in her way. Before all
else, Maggie Adams is a dancer.

An Avon Camelot Book   75366 • $1.75

"Some kids in our class act as though they can't wait to be teenagers. Some girls even wear green eye shadow to school and pierce their ears. I never want to grow up if that's how you're supposed to act."

The Trouble With Thirteen

by Betty Miles

Annie and her best friend Rachel wish they could stay twelve forever. Everything is perfect . . . until unexpected changes begin pulling them apart just when they need each other the most. But through it all, Annie and Rachel learn about independence and loyalty—and some good things about turning thirteen.

An Avon Camelot Book 51136 • $1.95

Also by Betty Miles:
JUST THE BEGINNING 55004 • $1.75
LOOKING ON 45898 • $1.75
THE REAL ME 55632 • $1.75